**Sometimes you have to make
sacrifices to get ahead . . .**

On Saturday, the group gathered in Cathy's garage. Paul's funeral had been a somber affair. No one could believe what had happened. Was bad luck doomed to follow Heart of Steel? It made Cathy's news all the more weird.

Cathy sat down behind her sound board. "Maybe this isn't the right time, guys, but I think we should talk about the future of the band."

"What band?" Jack said with a cynical laugh. We don't have any band."

Cathy took a deep breath. "This is going to sound strange, but we're more popular than ever. Since Paul—you know—well, all of a sudden we're the hottest band in town."

Wendy smiled. "I feel sort of creepy, but I think we should stick together. The only place to go from here is up."

Books in the Horror High series
Available from HarperPaperbacks

HORROR HIGH

Hard Rock

Nicholas Adams

HarperPaperbacks
A Division of HarperCollins*Publishers*

FOR LARRY KATZ

HarperPaperbacks *A Division of* HarperCollins*Publishers*
10 East 53rd Street, New York, N.Y. 10022

Produced by Daniel Weiss Associates, Inc.
33 West 17th Street, New York, New York 10011.

First printing: March, 1991

Printed in the United States of America

HarperPaperbacks and colophon are trademarks of HarperCollins*Publishers*

10 9 8 7 6 5 4 3 2 1

Chapter 1

Cathy Malone waited impatiently for the fifth-period bell to ring. The auburn-haired senior kept raising her blue eyes to the clock behind the instructor's desk. It was the last Friday of September, the day when the first issue of the *Cresswell Sentinel* went to press. Some of Cathy's hopes and dreams were riding on the publication of the school newspaper.

"Miss Malone?"

Cathy turned to regard Mr. Traxler, her senior English teacher. He was glaring at her. Cathy's smooth, white complexion turned redder than her short-cropped hair and her full lips. She sat there for a moment, silently looking back at Mr. Traxler.

The burly teacher folded his arms and stared down his thin nose at her. "Miss Malone, is something else on your mind? You seem to be preoccupied."

Cathy grimaced. "No, sir."

The rest of the class snickered and peered in her direction. Cathy had a reputation for being loose, offbeat, and punky. She certainly enhanced that image by dressing in torn jeans, a maroon tie-dyed T-shirt, a leather vest, motorcycle boots, and half-fingered leather gloves. She knew the more conventional kids would enjoy seeing her get into trouble.

Mr. Traxler smiled thinly. "So, Miss Malone, perhaps you'd like to offer your impression of today's lesson."

Cathy sighed and looked down at her desk. They had been studying "The Rime of the Ancient Mariner" all week. Cathy had read it twice. She kind of liked the poem. It was part fantasy, part science fiction.

"I'm waiting," Mr. Traxler intoned.

Cathy stiffened. "He messed up big time."

Mr. Traxler frowned uncertainly. "I beg your pardon?"

Cathy shrugged. "He really blew it, that mariner guy. You know, when he shot that bird with an arrow."

"Albatross," Mr. Traxler corrected. "Perhaps you'd like to elaborate for us, tell us how the Mariner 'blew it.' " He folded his arms, leaning back on the desk.

Cathy folded her own arms. "Sure. He got punished when he was on that ghost ship, after everybody died. You know, 'water, water everywhere and not a drop to drink.' That stuff. So now he's trying to warn everyone with all that stuff about 'He liveth best who loveth best' all the animals and stuff. He's telling everyone to show respect. That really ties in with today, doesn't it? I mean

2

with all this environmental junk. Maybe we should listen so we don't end up like him, and turn the planet into a ghost ship."

Mr. Traxler smiled a little. The class seemed to deflate with Cathy's triumph. Most of them hadn't even read the poem, much less formed an opinion about it. Cathy had disappointed everyone, except Mr. Traxler, by not flubbing the answer.

Mr. Traxler nodded approvingly. "Well, I'm pleasantly surprised, Miss Malone. Perhaps you'll—"

The bell rang to end fifth period. Cathy bolted quickly from her desk, running for the door. She hurried to her locker, switching books for sixth period. When she closed her locker, she turned to look for her boyfriend, Larry Hart.

"I hope you didn't mess it up for us," she muttered under her breath. "Come on, Larry, for once in your life . . ."

She sighed, wondering if she should have trusted Larry to carry out the errand. Larry had insisted that he take care of it. He wanted to show her that he really cared about their idea. They could pull it off together.

"Where are you, Larry?"

Suddenly she spotted him meandering down the hallway, swaggering as he approached. He was so fine—tall, slender, with thick shoulder-length black hair and bright green eyes. Like Cathy, he dressed funky in a denim jacket with the sleeves cut off, a white, V-necked T-shirt, patched jeans, and combat boots. A gold earring dangled from his left ear.

When he saw her, he waved and flashed his toothy, boyish smile. "Yo, Cat. What's doin'?"

He started to kiss her.

Cathy drew back. "Don't."

"What gives?"

Cathy looked into his eyes. "Larry, did you drop off that envelope like you said you would?"

Larry grimaced and turned away. "Uh-oh."

Cathy glared at him. "You forgot!"

"No, I just didn't—"

Her face turned red. "I told you that the deadline for all classified ads is the beginning of fifth period!"

"Cat, I—"

She exhaled and held out her hand. "Just give me the envelope. Maybe I can get them to take it anyway."

Larry put his hands on his hips. "Cat, I don't have it anymore."

"*What?*"

"Yeah, I had a problem in my shop class. I had to use the money for— Hey, Cat! Wait up!"

She had broken into a run, barreling down the hall. She had to make it to the newspaper office before they finalized the first issue. Cathy knew she shouldn't have trusted Larry. He was cute, talented, and a great kisser, but he wasn't very dependable.

Tearing up the stairs, she rounded the corner to see that the door was closed to the *Sentinel*'s office. Cathy banged on the door. After a moment, it swung open.

A ruddy-faced boy stuck his head out into the hall. "Yes, can I help you?"

"I want to put in a classified ad," Cathy replied. "I—"

The boy shook his head. "Sorry, you're too late. Try again next month." He started to close the door.

Cathy grabbed the door. "Please. It's important. I can't wait until next month."

"Sorry, we—"

A voice resounded from behind the boy. "Let her in. We can do it."

Reluctantly, he opened the door. Cathy pushed in to see a pleasant-looking woman sitting behind a huge cluttered desk. Her nameplate identified her as Mrs. Shirley. She was flanked by two female students who were busily shuffling stacks of paper.

"Hi," Cathy said apologetically. "I know I'm late, but I really have to get this ad in today."

Mrs. Shirley smiled and picked up a pencil. "Oh, it's all right. We need to flesh out the classified page anyway. What's your ad say, dear?"

Cathy took a deep breath. "Okay. It goes like this: 'Wanted. Singer, guitar, bass, and keyboard players for rock band. Heavy metal, mainstream, and reggae. Cover tunes and originals. Call Cathy, five-five-five-oh-two-three-eight.' That's it."

Mrs. Shirley counted the words. "That will be five dollars."

Cathy dug into her pockets. "Here, take this. Two dollars. I'll give you the rest on Monday."

Mrs. Shirley took the money and wrote out the receipt. "We'll trust you for it, Cathy. What's your last name?"

"Malone."

"All right. Here's your receipt. Balance due, three dollars. See you on Monday, dear."

Cathy smiled and breathed a sigh of relief. "Thanks, Mrs. Shirley. You're all right." She turned to leave.

"Cathy?" Mrs. Shirley called.

She wheeled around again. "Yes?"

"I was thinking of having someone write a music column for next month's paper. Are you interested?"

Cathy looked back at the two girls who flanked Mrs. Shirley. They were tense as they waited for Cathy's reply. They were clean-cut, Suzy-cream-cheese types from Rocky Bank Estates who lived in big houses, had fathers with good jobs, made the honor roll, went out for cheerleading. They looked down on girls like Cathy, who came from a single-parent home in the Upper Basin. They thought Cathy didn't belong with them, which suited Cathy fine. She didn't want to belong with them.

"Thanks for asking," Cathy replied. "But I'm not much of a writer. I'm more of a technical person, you know, sound equipment, special effects, stuff like that."

The nice girls breathed easier when Cathy turned it down.

Mrs. Shirley seemed disappointed. "Oh. Too bad. We could use a little spark in the *Sentinel*. Well, if you change your mind, you know where to find us, Cathy."

Cathy smiled warmly. "Thanks for taking my ad."

"You're welcome. Oh, one more thing. Don't you need a drummer for this rock band?"

Cathy shook her head. "No, my boyfriend is a great drummer. See you."

She went out into the hall. She barely made it to her Modern Media class before the tardy bell rang. This was another class she enjoyed.

After class, she hurried to her locker. A note was attached to its door. Cathy unfolded the piece of paper.

I'm sorry. I love you. Larry.

"You big jerk."

But she had to smile. Larry was irresistible, even if he was a goof-up. He had a rough, dangerous charm that made the other boys at Cresswell look like geeks. And underneath the tough exterior, he was really sort of childlike and insecure.

She knew where to find him. He was waiting for her on his motorcycle in the senior parking lot. As she approached him, he smiled weakly.

Cathy shook her head. "Hart, you lamebrain."

He grimaced. "Everything okay?"

Cathy touched the back of his hand. *He's such a hunk.* "Forget it, Lar. I got the ad in. It'll be out Monday. By Saturday, we'll be able to hold auditions."

"Yeah!" Larry said. "My babe! I knew you could do it. Hey, let's celebrate all weekend long."

"Saturday night," Cathy replied. "I have to study the rest of the weekend. You should, too."

"Not me. I'm a party boy."

"Larry, I mean it. . . ."

But he lowered his lips to hers, making Cathy forget about everything for the moment. Larry was a great kisser. It made up for some of his failings.

"Let's ride, Cat-girl."

She got on the back of his 750 Honda.

They roared through the streets of Cresswell with their hair flying in the breeze.

The weekend passed quickly for Cathy. On Saturday night, she and Larry rode his Honda to Porterville to go to a rock concert. They heard a group called the Charm Rangers, who played Top 40, with a definite bent toward heavy metal. Larry liked them but Cathy was critical of their sound. The mix wasn't right, which had something to do with the ego of the bass guitar player. He was obviously the leader of the group, and wanted his instrument to dominate. They sounded amateurish and uneven.

The next day was a rainy Sunday, so Cathy worked on her sound-control board. She had a workshop in back of her house. It was really just their old garage, but Cathy's mother never parked her car there, so Cathy had taken over and made it her sound station. She spent most of her free time there, studying circuits and working on various gadgets.

Cathy had been interested in rock music since her first concert at age twelve. In the beginning, she had been drawn to the musicians and their glamorous image. But when she was fourteen, she had won backstage passes for a really hot band. That's where she had first seen the "techies," the men and women behind the scenes who made the show come together. After that, Cathy had been fascinated with all of the technical aspects that went into producing sounds.

It had taken Cathy most of the summer to piece together the crude but effective sound mixing board. She had gotten different components of systems that she had found in the junk bins of music and audio stores. Some of the equipment had also come from flea markets and yard sales. Larry had helped her a little, but he wasn't that interested in it. He only wanted to bang his drums, which was fine with Cathy, since he usually only got in her way, anyway.

Cathy couldn't wait to mix the sounds of her own group. She dreamed of becoming a well-known engineer and recording expert. But first she had to assemble a band, find her starting point. And that would happen as soon as the *Cresswell Sentinel* came out on Monday.

* * *

"Yo, Cat!"

Cathy looked up from her locker to see Larry rushing down the hall, waving a copy of the *Sentinel*. Cathy closed her locker and turned toward him.

"Is the ad in there?" she asked.

Larry shrugged. "I dunno. I haven't looked yet. I figured you'd want to see it as soon as it got here."

"Here, take my books."

Larry grabbed the books, trapping them against his chest. "Chill out, Cat. It's gonna be cool."

Cathy snatched the paper from him and opened it to the classified ads. Her eyes went down the page. When she saw it, she smiled for a moment. Then her eyes narrowed and her face took on an expression of anger and disbelief.

"No!"

Larry frowned, trying to look over her shoulder. "What is it?"

"This is horrible!" Cathy cried. "Just horrible!"

Chapter 2

Larry squinted at the ad. "I don't see anything wrong."

Cathy shook her head. "Those *witches!* Those demons from— Oh, wait till I get my hands on them!"

"On who?" Larry asked.

"Milli and Vanilli," Cathy replied. "The gorgons of Cresswell High."

Larry laughed. "I still don't know what you're talking about."

"When I placed the ad, there were two girls in the newspaper office," Cathy said. "Real straight types, you know, the kind who think heavy metal is something that goes into their braces."

"Oh. Yeah? What'd they do?"

Cathy slapped the paper. "They got the ad wrong. Look at this. My phone number is wrong. See? Two-oh-eight-three. My number is oh-two-three-eight. They did it on purpose. I know it. I watched Mrs. Shirley write it down myself."

Larry frowned. "Why would they do something like that?"

"Because I'm cool and they're not," Cathy replied. "They can't stand anyone who's different."

Larry shrugged. "Ah, don't sweat it. We can put up posters on the bulletin board."

Cathy wadded up the newspaper in a ball. "I even went by to pay Mrs. Shirley that three dollars this morning. What jerks. Now we're going to have to wait a whole month before we can put in another ad."

Larry put his hand on her shoulder. "Aw, don't blow a fuse, Cat. It's not that bad."

"Oh, come on," Cathy replied. "Walk me to class. Maybe we can think of something else."

"Sure," Larry replied.

Jack Akers watched as Cathy Malone and her boyfriend walked toward him. Jack had a crush on Cathy, but he was a wrestler, a jock. Cathy always went for the funky, motorcycle guys like Larry Hart. Jack had been wanting to get up the nerve to talk to Cathy, and now the ad in the school paper had presented a perfect opportunity.

Jack took a deep breath. His muscular chest pushed against the fabric of his Cresswell T-shirt. He had broad shoulders and thick arms from weight training. His long blond hair hung over his ears.

As Cathy and Larry came closer, Jack hesitated. He had never been good at talking to girls, but he had to take a shot if he was going to meet

Cathy. He was just going to have to act cool, tough.

He stepped away from his locker and called to them. "Hey, you!"

Cathy and Larry turned to look at him. Larry stepped in front of Cathy, and a hostile expression spread over his face.

"You got a problem, dude?" Larry asked.

Jack smirked at him. "Yeah, I got a lot of problems, but they don't have anything to do with you. I want to talk to the chick."

Cathy stepped around from behind Larry. "I'm not a chick, I'm a woman. What's your problem?"

Jack blushed. He wondered if he had blown it already. Cathy was so beautiful, even with an angry look on her face.

"Are you Cathy?" he asked.

"Yeah. Who wants to know?"

Jack thrust the copy of the *Sentinel* toward her. "This your ad?"

Cathy nodded as she sized up the brawny guy in front of her. His T-shirt said that he was on the Cresswell High wrestling team. He was really built.

Larry glared at Jack. "You a jock?"

"Yeah," Jack replied. "But I play bass too. My name is Jack Akers. I want to try out for the band."

Larry shook his head. "I don't know—"

Cathy poked Larry in the ribs. "Of course he can try out. Here, let me give you my real phone number. The one in the paper is bogus. Typographical error."

Jack watched her write down the phone number. His heart was pounding. He wished that Larry would get lost so he could talk to Cathy alone.

"Call me tonight," Cathy said. "We're going to set up auditions."

"Thanks," Jack replied, smiling. "Will do."

"Great," Cathy said. "Later, Jack."

As they moved off down the hall, Jack saw Larry lean closer to Cathy, whispering something. Jack clenched his fist and raised it in the air. Jack had done it. He was going to get his chance with her. They were pretty different, but Jack was willing to give it a shot. He couldn't believe his good luck. He moved off down the hall, swaggering triumphantly.

"Cathy, Cathy" he said to himself. "Looking fine."

"I don't think I like that guy," Larry said. "He's too cocky."

Cathy winked at him. "Sounds like somebody else I know."

"Huh?"

The tardy bell rang.

"See you after school," Cathy said.

"Yeah, sure."

Cathy ducked into her class. She had already lined up one hopeful band member. And there would be plenty more before the day ended.

Darren Quick sat in his American history class, looking at the ad in the *Cresswell Sentinel.* He pushed back the thick glasses that had fallen down on his nose.

Darren had played the organ since he was ten years old, but he had never been in a rock band. He had played at church and for one musical production during his sophomore year. With his alligator shirt and his short hair, he seemed more likely to make the honor roll than to slam chords in a rock group.

"Darren?"

He looked up quickly at his teacher. "Yes, Miss Hargreave?"

"What are you reading?" she asked.

"Uh, my notes," Darren replied. "From today's lesson."

"All right, then. Can you answer the questions I've written on the board?"

Darren peered through his thick lenses. "Uh, yes, ma'am. Jefferson Davis was the president of the Confederacy, and the Battle of Gettysburg was probably the turning point in the Civil War."

Miss Hargreave smiled appreciatively. "Very good, Darren."

Two girls snickered behind him. Darren was sure he heard the word "wimp" whispered. Someone had called him a "dweeb" on the school bus that morning. He was a good student and a nice guy, but Darren didn't have the image to be popular.

His eyes focused on the ad again. They needed a keyboard player. Rock and roll couldn't be any harder than the Bach fugues he had been playing. He could pick up the songs. He had a good ear.

"I'm going to do it," he muttered to himself.

The girls behind him laughed again. Darren blushed. They'd be singing a different tune when he was a rock star. Then he would have the last laugh.

Cathy grimaced and waved her hands in the air. "Okay, that's it. You can stop now."

A dark-haired girl had been singing a horrible, off-key rendition of "Purple Rain." She kept singing for a few moments, and finally Cathy had to switch off her microphone from the sound board.

"Hey, what happened?"

"I pulled the plug," Cathy replied.

The girl began to pop gum in her mouth. "So, do I get the gig? I mean, I sounded pretty good, huh?"

Cathy forced a smile. It was a cool Saturday in more ways than one. The whole week had been spent lining up prospective musicians and singers. Since ten o'clock that morning, Cathy had been listening to a horde of auditioners, with mixed results.

"What's the deal?" the singer asked.

"Uh, we've got your number," Cathy replied. "We'll give you a call."

The girl stormed out of Cathy's garage in a huff.

Larry came out from behind his drum set and walked toward Cathy with a half-smile on his lips. He was tired of listening to people who couldn't carry a tune in a bucket.

"Looks pretty grim," he said.

Cathy glanced toward the makeshift stage. "Well, it's not all that bad. We've got Jack and Darren."

Larry nodded. "Yeah, the muscle-boy can play. He knows a lot of songs and he can pick up on style."

"Darren seems to know what he's doing, too," Cathy offered. "He's good."

The preppie had been a real surprise. He didn't look like a rocker, but he was the best keyboard player to audition. His fingers had flown across the electric organ.

"We still need a guitarist and a singer," Cathy said.

Larry took a deep breath. "Okay, let's keep going. Who's next?"

A guitar player and a singer came in from outside and joined Larry, Jack, and Darren on stage. But as soon as they started to play, it was clear that they didn't have what it takes. Cathy sent them packing.

Jack Akers looked over at her and Larry. "What's doing, Cathy? I mean, am I in the band or what?"

Jack was nervous. He really wanted to be in the

group, but Cathy wasn't ready to give him the okay. To be fair, she had to audition everyone before the permanent roles were cast.

"Can you wait awhile, Jack?"

He smiled softly. "Sure, anything for you, Cathy."

Larry didn't like his sweet tone. "Why don't you take a break, Akers? We all need one."

Jack looked coldly at Larry, then unplugged his bass, left the stage, and stalked out of the garage.

"Larry," Cathy said, "don't be like that."

Darren looked down at her. "Uh, Miss Malone . . ."

"You sounded great, Darren," Cathy replied. "Give us a minute, okay?"

"Sure."

Darren started outside. His stomach was turning. He knew he had a chance, but it was still up in the air.

When they were alone, Larry took Cathy's hands. "You wanna keep going with this?"

Cathy sighed. "I guess so. If we don't find a singer and a lead guitar, we're hopeless."

She could see her dream going down the tubes. Surely there were two more rockers at Cresswell High. But when they started up the auditions again, Cathy's spirits sunk even lower.

Todd Steele drove his Chevy van through the tree-lined streets of Rocky Bank Estates. He was late for the audition, and he had to pick up his girlfriend, Wendy Coles. Todd hated coming into this fancy neighborhood. With his beat-up van and his long hair, the cops were always stopping him for no reason.

Wendy was waiting for Todd outside her two-story house. She was a tall blond girl with incredible hazel eyes. She was wearing a leotard top and blue jeans that showed off her great figure. Sometimes Todd couldn't believe that a girl like Wendy had gone for him.

As he pulled the van over to the curb, Wendy came running toward him. She got in and kissed him lightly on the lips.

Todd smiled at her. "We're late."

"Sorry," she replied. "I—"

"It's not your fault. You sure you don't mind going with me while I audition for this group?"

"Er, no. In fact, if I can get up the nerve, I'd like to audition myself. Would you mind?"

"No way. I'd love for us to be in the same group. It's just that . . ."

She turned her devastating eyes on him. "What?"

"Well, I mean, rock-and-roll bands can get kind of raunchy sometimes. You might not—"

"It's okay," Wendy replied sweetly. "I'm not a daisy—I won't wilt. Besides, I just said that I *might* audition. I'm not even sure I want to, but I've been singing some on my own. I thought it might be fun."

"Go for it."

Wendy put her hand on his arm. "You're great, Todd."

He laughed and looked away. "I don't know about that."

"What's wrong?" Wendy asked.

"Uh, there are some things you don't know about me, Wendy. I mean, we've only been going out a couple of weeks, and I think I should . . ."

"Is this about that trouble you were in?" Wendy asked quickly.

Todd shot a sideways glance at her. "Yeah! How did you—"

"I heard about it," Wendy replied. "Some of my girlfriends were trying to warn me." She laughed lightly.

"What'd they say?" Todd could feel the sweat break out on his forehead. If he lost Wendy now . . .

"Just that you were with some boys who stole a car, and had to go away for a while. Some kind of reform school."

Todd felt himself trembling. "It was a bad rap, Wendy. I swear. All of that's history now."

She smiled warmly. "Forget it. I didn't know you then. Hey, aren't we late for that audition?"

"Yeah, we better get going."

They left Rocky Bank Estates, heading for the Upper Basin. It took a while to find Cathy's house. When they finally arrived, Wendy suddenly got cold feet, and didn't want to audition. She told Todd she would wait in the van while he went in and played for Cathy Malone.

* * *

"Well," Cathy said. "That's it. No lead singer and no guitarist. I guess we're sunk."

Larry shook his head and threw down his drumsticks. "Bad scene, man."

Jack Akers frowned. If the band didn't take off, he wouldn't get to hang around with Cathy. He'd never have a chance with her.

Darren was bummed out too. He had survived the audition process, but what good would that do if he didn't get into a band? Nerd-boy would live forever.

"Yo!" a voice called from the back of the garage. "Am I too late?"

They all turned toward the guy in the heavy-metal costume. He had sprawling brown hair and glitter boots. He carried a fake-lizard guitar case in his right hand.

"Do you play guitar?" Cathy asked.

"Yeah. The name's Steele. Todd Steele. Sorry I'm late."

Cathy and Larry exchanged glances. Larry shrugged. He was ready to try anything to keep the band alive.

Cathy nodded toward the stage. "Plug in, Todd. Let's see what you can do."

As Todd tuned his guitar, he told them that he had already been in one band. He neglected to tell them that it had been a band at the state correctional facilities for juvenile offenders. He also mentioned that he had composed about twenty of his own songs if the group wanted to do original material. He could get the job done.

"Okay," Cathy said. "Give us a solo, Todd."

Without hesitation, Todd struck a pose. His fingers began to move quickly, sliding across the neck of the Ibanez guitar. Everyone was stunned. He was tons better than the other guitar players who had auditioned.

Cathy waved her hands. "Okay, stop."

Todd came to a halt, frowning at her. "What's wrong?"

Cathy smiled at him. "Nothing. You're great! Why don't you all try a song together? How about 'Wild Thing'? Do you know it, Todd?"

"Sure." He looked at Larry and the others. "I'm ready."

Larry clicked his drumsticks together. "One, two . . ."

Cathy worked with her sound board as they played the song. They weren't exactly tight, but they were better than any combination that had been tried that day. When they were finished, they all turned to see Cathy looking unenthusiastic.

"What's wrong?" Todd asked. "Was I bad?"

He realized suddenly how desperately he wanted to get into the group. There was almost nothing that he loved more than playing his guitar. It would help him put his delinquent past behind him. But he didn't like the look on Cathy's face.

"You were fine," Cathy replied. "But we really need a singer. I mean, Larry has a good voice—he can carry some of the heavier tunes. But my ear tells me that we need the balance of a female voice."

Todd looked hopefully at Cathy. "Uh, I think I know someone."

"Really?" Cathy replied. "Can she come today?"

Todd put down his guitar. "Gimme a minute."

He hurried out of the garage. In a few minutes he returned with Wendy, who came in timidly and smiled weakly at Cathy.

"This is Wendy Coles," Todd said. "She wants to audition."

Larry struck a cymbal on his drum set. "Whoa. Come right in, babe. Pull up a microphone and sit down."

Cathy shot a nasty look at Larry. "Down, boy. Let's see if she can sing first."

"Who cares?" Larry said. "Foxy lady!"

Jack smiled. *Watch it, Larry,* he thought. Maybe this was his chance to move in.

"Party hearty," Larry kept on. "If she sings half as good as she looks, she'll sound great."

Wendy ignored Larry's leer. "Listen, if there's a problem—"

"No," Cathy replied. "Pick up the microphone."

Cathy watched skeptically as Wendy walked up onto the stage. She felt a twinge of jealousy at the blond girl's incredible looks. But she didn't want to judge Wendy by her appearance. That would make her as bad as the girls who had sabotaged her ad.

Darren and Todd were also staring at Wendy with adoration.

Wendy's husky voice floated through the garage. "I've never sung with a group before."

Larry played a suggestive cadence on his drums. "You'll do fine, sweet thing."

I'm sure she will, Cathy thought. *But she better keep it to singing.*

Wendy looked over her shoulder. "Do you know 'I Can't Wait'?"

Todd winked and nodded. "No problem."

Larry ran his sticks over the tom-toms. "You got it, gorgeous."

"I know that one," Jack said. "Darren?"

Darren frowned. "What's the chord progression?"

"G, A-minor, C, and F on the break," Todd replied.

Darren shrugged. "You take it, I'll follow."

Wendy cleared her throat and lifted the microphone to her lips. "Ah one, two, three . . ."

The band broke into the song. It was rough at first, but then Wendy began to sing. Immediately, the band sounded better. Cathy worked with the dials on the sound board. By the end of the song, the band had found some cohesion that had not been there before.

Cathy applauded when the song ended. "All right! Not bad. Wendy, are you sure you never sang with a band before?"

"No," Wendy replied. "I just sing around the house."

Larry raised his drumsticks. "She's our number-one babe!"

Cathy glared at him. Everyone was quiet for a moment. It was clear that Cathy was getting fed up with Larry's flirting.

"Uh, you guys," Cathy said tightly. "Would you mind waiting outside a minute? Not you, Larry. You stay here."

Darren, Todd, Wendy, and Jack shot quick glances at each other, then stepped off the stage and headed outside.

"I hope I'm in," Darren Quick said to Jack.

Jack didn't hear him. If he made it into the group, he was sure he could take Cathy away from that idiot Larry. How could Larry even look at anyone else when Cathy was around?

Todd and Wendy stood together, leaning against the garage door.

"I'm sure you made it," Wendy said to Todd. "But I don't know about me. I don't think Cathy liked me."

Jack turned to look at Wendy. "Aw, she's nice. She wouldn't hold it against you because Larry was acting like a jerk."

"How was I?" Darren asked.

Todd smiled. "You were okay, Quick. Not bad at all."

Darren frowned slightly. Did Todd mean it? Was he just setting him up? If Darren didn't get into the band, he was doomed forever to his nerdhood. He would never overcome the wimpy image that made girls snicker behind his back.

"It'll be great," Todd whispered to Wendy. "I'll be a rock and roller, not some kid who stole a car."

Wendy gazed off dreamily into space. "Gosh, what if we really made it big? I mean, we could get out of Cresswell."

"You've already got it made," Todd replied. "You live in Rocky Bank Estates."

"Not for long," Wendy told him quietly. "My father was laid off last week at the bank. We're going to lose the house if he doesn't find a job."

Todd frowned at her. "Why didn't you tell me about this?"

"I was embarrassed," she whispered. "I—"

Someone pushed on the garage door. Todd and Wendy moved out of the way. Everyone seemed to tighten up. Had the final verdict arrived?

Cathy stuck her head through the opening. "Okay, everyone inside."

They filed in silently. Larry was sitting behind his drums with a glum look on his face. He winked and grinned when he saw Wendy. Wendy ignored him, taking Todd's arm.

"Well," Cathy said pleasantly. "How about it? Would you all like to be in the group?"

"Yeah!" Jack cried. Impulsively, he leaned over and squeezed Cathy's shoulder.

Darren smiled broadly. He could just see the looks on those girls' faces—the girls who had laughed at him. He could even grow his hair longer and start dressing a little wilder.

Todd gave Wendy a kiss. They were both grinning. It was official!

Wendy looked at Cathy. "I won't let you down, Cathy. Thanks."

"Rock on!" Cathy replied. "Looks like we have ourselves a band."

They celebrated by going out for burgers. On the way to the restaurant, Cathy noticed the way Larry kept looking at Wendy. But she told herself not to be jealous. If the band was going to work, she had to act professionally.

There was no way she could have anticipated the kind of trouble that would begin at the very first rehearsal.

Chapter 3

Cathy stood at her sound-mixing board with her hands on the controls. "Okay," she said to the group. "Sound check. Darren, you kick it off."

Darren Quick adjusted his glasses and put his hands over the keys of his electronic organ. He played a G chord for Cathy. Her blue eyes watched the digital readout. She brought up the volume a little, listening as the sound came out of a large speaker.

"Great, Darren," she said. "Todd, let me hear a riff."

Todd Steele crouched into an affected pose, running his fingers up and down the neck of his guitar. His whole body shook as the wailing sound rose in Cathy's garage. The readout almost went off the meter. She had to turn it down to keep the speakers from blowing.

Cathy gave Todd an enthusiastic high sign. "Hot stuff, Steele!"

Todd grinned. "Hey, I can do it again."

Cathy shook her head. "Save it for rehearsal. Wendy, try your mike, and then let's hear the guitar."

Wendy Coles had an old Fender Stratocaster slung over her shoulder. In addition to being Todd's girlfriend and having a great voice, she could also play rhythm guitar. Cathy had been surprised to find out that Wendy was so talented. Her good looks and the extra guitar were an unbeatable combination. Wendy was a real find.

Wendy leaned closer to the microphone. She spoke a few words and then slammed a hard C chord. She smiled. This was what she had been born to do—meeting Cathy had been a stroke of luck. With Cathy's technical expertise, Wendy had never sounded better. Cathy could make her a star.

Cathy looked up at Jack Akers. "Let's hear that bass."

Jack grinned. "I've been working on a reggae riff. Check it out."

Jack began to play a slow, primal bass line. As Cathy adjusted the sound level, the other members of the band kicked in, following Jack. They jammed for a moment until Cathy waved her hands to tell them to stop.

"Sounds great," she told them. "We're all set."

Wendy glanced back at the empty drum set. "Except for Larry."

Todd frowned. "Yeah, where is he, anyway?"

"He's late," Jack said expressionlessly. "Real late."

Darren pushed his glasses back on his nose. "We can't get started without him. Cathy?"

She sighed and stepped back from her sound

board. She had been worried about the other members of the band, but Larry was the one who hadn't arrived on time for the first rehearsal. It was a Monday evening, two days after the Saturday audition. They only had a couple of hours to practice. If they played too late, the neighbors would complain.

"Where's your boyfriend?" Jack asked Cathy.

"Didn't he know about the rehearsal?" Todd added.

"He knew," Cathy replied, looking at the clock on the board. "I hope nothing has happened to him. Maybe I should give him a call."

"Good idea," Todd said. "I'm ready to play."

Wendy nodded. "Yeah, we have a lot of songs to learn."

Cathy felt embarrassed about Larry's tardiness. After all, it was *their* band. As one of the leaders of the group, Larry had to set an example. She started for the garage door, but before she could reach it, it began to open.

Cathy put her hands on her hips. "Well, it's about time you—oh . . ."

The oval face that peeked through the open door wasn't Larry's. Instead, a young, dark-haired girl came into the garage. She wore a tight wool skirt that barely covered her hips. A red blouse, leather jacket, and mesh stockings were an obvious attempt to look older on the girl's part. But she was pretty. Her face was framed by thick, jet-black hair that shimmered when she moved.

"Hi, Cathy," she said in a sweet voice.

Cathy frowned at her. "Margo, what are you doing here?"

"I—I don't know, I just—"

"Who is this?" Jack asked.

"Margo Reardon," Cathy replied.

Margo smiled weakly. She was wearing too much makeup. Her full lips were glistening with a fiery red hue. Rouge brought her cheeks to life.

"Margo's my next-door neighbor," Cathy went on. "We're about to rehearse, Margo. Why don't you come back later?"

Margo didn't seem to hear her. "I just wondered if you needed any help over here. I heard the music and—"

"I don't think we need any help," Cathy said. "We have to—"

Margo stepped past her, looking up at Wendy. "Hey, you're Wendy Coles. I've seen you at Cresswell. I go there, you know. I'm a sophomore."

Cathy shook her head. She barely tolerated Margo's pushiness. Margo came from one of those strange families that sometimes gave the Upper Basin a bad name. She had to get rid of her so they could practice.

Margo looked back at Cathy with her wide, brown eyes. "Please let me stay, Cathy. I won't get in the way. I'll help you. I'll do anything you say. I promise. Please."

Cathy felt bad, but she didn't want Margo around. "We're busy here, Margo. It's our first rehearsal."

"Please, Cathy. I just want to watch. I won't make any noise."

"Margo—"

"Please!"

"Aw, let her stay, Cat!"

They all looked toward the door. Larry stood there with his drumsticks in hand. He was smiling at Margo, who immediately smiled back.

Margo's red lips parted slightly. "I know you! You're Larry Hart. You ride a motorcycle."

"You're also late!" Cathy said. "We've been ready for half an hour."

Larry shrugged, keeping his eyes on Margo. "Hey, I'm a few minutes late. Big deal. Who's the babe?"

"I'm Margo. Margo Reardon. Wow, you look fine, Larry. Like a real heavy-metal drummer."

"You look okay, too, Margo," Larry replied. "So, gang, how's it shaking?"

Cathy shot him a hostile look and turned back to her sound board. "Get behind your drums, Larry. We've got work to do."

Larry squinted at her. "Chill out. Who died and left you boss?"

An awkward silence fell over the garage. The other members of the group were looking uncomfortably at Larry. The rehearsal was already off to a bad start.

Wendy looked a little angry. "We've all been waiting for you, Larry," she said impatiently.

Larry walked over to her and put his arm around her shoulder. He gave her a little peck on the cheek, rubbing his hand up and down her back.

"I bet you've been waiting for me, babe," Larry said. "You're looking pretty fine, Wendo."

Todd bristled. "Come on, Hart. Shake it up. We haven't got all night."

Larry winked at Wendy. "I wouldn't say that. All night is where it's at. Right, gorgeous?"

Cathy's jaw dropped. She couldn't believe that Larry was doing this. And he didn't let up.

"Hey, Wendy," he said suggestively, "you like to stay up late?"

Todd took a step toward Larry. "That's enough, Hart!"

Larry wheeled, puffing out his chest. "Yeah? How's that?"

Todd pointed a finger at him. "You're pushing it."

"I guess you'd know all about pushing it," Larry replied. "You found out when you and your buddies stole that car!"

Todd took off his guitar and started toward Larry. "That's it!"

Larry egged him on. "Let's do it, Steele. I'm not afraid of you."

Cathy turned to Jack. "Stop them!"

Jack nodded. Personally, he kind of wanted to see Larry get his butt kicked, but if Cathy didn't want them to fight, he would stop them.

"You're mine!" Todd said to Larry, pushing back his sleeves.

Jack quickly stepped between them. "That's it, boys. Fight's over."

Todd tried to push around him. "Hart's got it coming!"

"No!" Cathy cried.

Jack grabbed Todd's shoulders and pushed him back. "Hey, Cathy doesn't want anyone fighting. Back off, Steele."

"Chicken!" Larry said. "He's afraid I'm going to steal his girl."

"Don't flatter yourself," Wendy said.

Larry threw out his hands. "Hey, lighten up."

Jack turned to face Larry. "No, *you* lighten up, Hart. What's your problem? You've got Cathy upset."

"I wouldn't let that bother you," Larry replied.

"It does," Jack said. "It bothers all of us."

Larry made a face and turned away. Everyone was tense, waiting to see what would happen. Cathy was hurt and angry, but Larry wouldn't even look at her. Instead, he turned to Margo and smiled.

Margo adoringly gazed back at him. "Wow, I'd love to hear you play, Larry."

Larry took Margo's hand. "Come on, you can sit next to me, doll."

He led Margo toward the drum set and eased down on the stool. Margo sat off to the side, smiling like a dutiful groupie.

Everyone took a deep breath. They were looking to Cathy for guidance. She was fighting the urge to cry.

"All right," she said a little shakily. "Let's see if we can get started."

They moved to their places. Jack lingered for a moment, staring at Cathy. She caught the concerned look in his eyes.

"It's okay, Jack," she said.

He smiled weakly. "I'm sorry, Cathy. If you need me to—"

"No, go on. Let's get rehearsal started. Try one song. Does everyone know 'Glass House'?"

Everyone knew it. They didn't look at Larry as he banged his sticks together and started the number. Cathy tried to forget her seething emotions as they started to play.

In spite of Larry's attitude, the group seemed natural together. They got through the rehearsal, learning five songs in the process. At the end of the evening, Larry left without saying a word to anyone. Margo followed him out.

Cathy wondered why Larry was being such a dink. His talent had gone to his head. She was so embarrassed at the way he had come on to Wendy right there in front of everyone.

"Not bad," she told the others.

Darren was bright red, not sure what to say. "Uh, when's our next rehearsal, Cathy?"

"Saturday," she replied.

Todd shook his head. "I can't believe the way Hart acted. What a dweeb!"

Wendy sighed. "Yeah, he's on a star trip. But he's a good drummer. The band sounded great tonight."

Jack had moved over next to Cathy. "Hey, are you all right?" he said, touching her shoulder.

Cathy nodded and shrugged away from him. Jack bit back his impatience. He wanted to take care of Cathy. Surely she couldn't be hung up on Larry after the way he had treated her.

"Are you sure you're all right?" Jack asked.

"Yeah," Cathy replied. "Don't worry about me."

Jack wanted to take her into his arms and kiss her. He knew she would feel the same way about him if she would only let herself forget Larry. He knew it.

"Don't worry about tonight," Cathy said. "We'll straighten it out on Saturday."

"Sure we will," Jack said with a smile.

But at the next rehearsal, things only got worse.

"He's late again," Jack said, looking at his watch. "What a geek."

Cathy let out a disgusted sigh. They were all assembled in her garage for the second rehearsal. Cathy had already taken a sound check, but Larry was pulling his disappearing act again.

Darren, whose hopes of stardom were rapidly dwindling, shook his head. "What's wrong with him? I mean, he's not a bad drummer. . . ."

"He could be replaced," Todd said. "He's not *that* good."

Wendy looked at Cathy. "How about it? Should we start without him?"

Cathy nodded. She didn't feel like defending her boyfriend. There was no reason for him to show such disrespect for the other members of the group.

"I'll have to talk to him," she said. "If he—"

She broke off when she heard Larry's Honda pulling up outside the garage.

"His royal highness arrives," Jack muttered under his breath.

Why is Cathy even giving him a break? Jack thought. She deserved better. Jack could teach Larry a lesson. He had no right to be such a prima donna. "Cathy, I could talk to Larry for you. I could show him what's what."

"No," Cathy replied. "I'll do it after rehearsal."

They all waited for Larry to enter. When he walked into the garage, Cathy's mouth dropped open. Margo was hanging on Larry's arm. She let go when she saw Cathy glaring at her.

"Hi," Margo said meekly.

Cathy pointed toward the door. "Out, Margo. This is a private rehearsal."

"She can stay," Larry said bluntly. "I just gave her a ride. She was hitching from downtown."

Jack's face was red. He wanted to bash in Larry's skull. Cathy was too special to be treated like this.

Cathy glared at Larry. "We're all waiting for you. Is it that hard to be on time?"

Larry put his hands on his hips. "You're acting like a real b—"

Wendy grabbed her microphone. "Break time, students. Let's take five while the lovers quarrel."

Cathy waved her hand in the air. "No. Let's rehearse. That's what we came here for."

Larry slid his arm around Margo's shoulder. "Come on, honey. You can watch a real pro in action."

"Real pros aren't late," Jack said dryly.

Larry shot him a hostile look. He could tell that Jack was ready to fight, but Larry backed down, taking his place behind the drums. Margo sat on the edge of the stage.

Cathy hovered over her sound board, seething inside. Why was Larry doing this to her? What was going on with Margo anyway? She took a deep breath, trying to overcome her anger. She wasn't going to let her personal problems get in the way of the group's progress.

Larry hit the snare drum a couple of times. No one looked at him except Margo. Her bright red lips were parted in a smile.

Cathy couldn't resist throwing a barb in Larry's direction. "All right, let's kick it off with 'Two Timer.' Everyone know that one?"

Larry's eyes narrowed. Cathy smiled. He had understood the dig. Everyone else was smiling, too.

"Good choice," Jack said, grinning at Cathy.

Darren laughed. "What's the chord progression?"

"L and M," Todd said. "Oh, no, wait a minute. It's D, G, and F, with A-minor on the break."

"Give *me* a break," Larry said.

"What's the matter?" Jack challenged. "Can't keep up, Larry? Maybe if you made it to rehearsal on time . . ."

Larry turned bright red. He was angry, but he didn't want to tangle with Jack. Cathy had nailed him with the song choice.

"I don't want to do 'Two Timer,' " Larry said.

"Aw, that's too bad," Cathy replied. "Jack, kick it off."

Jack smiled and winked at her. "Uh one, two, uh one-two-three!"

"Okay," Cathy said, taking off her headphones. "Sounds good, campers!"

The rehearsal had gone well, despite the shaky beginning. They had added three more songs to their repertoire. Some of the tension had eased while they were playing.

Larry leaned back on his stool. "Yeah, it was pretty good, even if I do say so myself."

Jack rolled his eyes. "Gimme a break."

Margo waved at Larry from the back of the garage. "Hot, guys. Really . . ."

Cathy turned to glare at her. "Take a break, Margo. I've got to talk to the band. It's business. You understand."

Margo frowned, looking to Larry for support, but Larry waved her out. He knew Cathy was at the breaking point. Margo slinked away like a scolded puppy.

Cathy looked at the band. "Listen up, guys.

You're sounding better all the time. I think we're ready for our first gig."

Wendy smiled at Cathy, her eyes wide. *"Really?"*

"A gig?" Jack wondered aloud. "Wow! We've only been playing together for a week."

Larry squinted from behind his drums. "Gig? This is the first I've heard of it. Why didn't you say something, Cat?"

"Why don't you come to rehearsal on time?" Cathy asked.

Darren had a smile on his face. "You mean we're going to play in front of people?" At last, he would get some recognition! This would blow people away!

"Maybe," Cathy replied. "We have to audition first."

"We don't even know ten songs!" Larry argued.

Cathy ignored him. "It's only a junior-high dance," she went on. "It's a week away. We can add a few more songs by then. Those seventh- and eighth-graders won't know the difference. Besides, it pays enough for us to buy some more sound equipment."

"Junior high!" Larry said loudly. "That's bogus."

Wendy shrugged, taking Cathy's side. "I don't know. Maybe she's right. Junior high might not be so bad."

"We have to audition?" Todd asked.

"If we want the gig," Cathy replied. "I can

have the student council president come here and listen to us."

Larry got up and started for the door. "Hey, Cat, I'm not playing any stupid junior-high gig. Put it in your hat."

"Where are you going?" Jack said to Larry.

"To make sure Margo is all right," Larry replied. "Cathy hurt her feelings."

Larry stormed out of the garage.

"What a jerk," Todd said.

Jack exhaled. "Man, he's really gone." *And Cathy's still hung up on him.*

Wendy laughed. "No, he's just in love with himself."

Cathy fought back the negative emotions that burned inside her. "He'll come around. In the meantime, what do you say? Are we going to play the junior-high dance or not?"

"What about Mr. Wonderful?" Jack asked.

"I'll have a talk with him," Cathy replied, though she wasn't sure how to do it. "We can vote without him. Majority rules."

Wendy nodded. "I'd dig it. A live gig."

Jack laughed. "Why not? They're only junior-high kids."

Todd struck a lick on his guitar. "A live gig! I'll make their eardrums bleed!"

Cathy looked toward the keyboard player. "Darren?"

"Hey, I'm ready to go," he replied confidently. "I need some new clothes, though."

"Okay," Cathy said. "Then we're on. I'll set up

41

the audition for the next practice. We sound good enough."

As the others left, Cathy thought things were looking up. Of course, she had to deal with Larry, but she could handle him. At least, she thought so until she went outside to lock up the garage.

While she was fiddling with the old combination lock, Cathy heard a strange sound coming from the side of the garage. She hesitated, listening to the lilt of human voices.

Cathy turned away from the door and saw that Larry's Honda was still parked in her backyard. Her heart began to pound. She inched her way toward the side of the garage.

A soft moaning noise rose in the air. Cathy heard voices, but she couldn't make out the words coming from the alley. She drew closer.

"Larry, I love you. You're so fine."

Cathy stopped dead in her tracks. *Margo!* Her face flushed red. *That little tramp!* Cathy heard them kissing.

Larry's voice echoed in the alley. "You've got to prove it, Margo. I mean, I've got a good thing going with Cathy. I don't want to blow it if I'm not going to do better. Know what I mean?"

You just blew it—big time! Cathy thought.

She heard more kissing. She leaned around the corner to see them standing in the shadows. Margo was against the wall. Larry pressed his body into hers. His hands were all over her.

Cathy drew back, choking on tears. Her throat had constricted. How could Larry do this to her?

What a supreme jerk. She felt like killing them both.

"I can give you what you want," Margo said. "You know I love you, Larry."

"When?"

That sleaze!

"Soon," Margo replied. "But you have to drop her, Larry. I don't want to be your second girl."

Right here in my own backyard!

"Don't talk about Cathy," Larry replied. "She'll stay out of our way. But I need to know where I stand with you, Margo."

The little sophomore tramp! And Larry wasn't any better. He had asked Cathy to go steady with him, but he was already cheating on her.

"Does Cathy give you what you want?" Margo asked.

Larry just grunted.

"I didn't think so," Margo replied. "Behind all that leather and denim, she's a good girl."

"Margo—"

Cathy tensed. Maybe Larry was going to leave. If he walked away from Margo now, Cathy might be able to forgive him. She held her breath.

"I can give you what you want," Margo said in a low voice. "What you need. You know that, Larry."

Cathy crossed her fingers.

"Hush," Larry said. "Cathy might hear us."

"Kiss me, Larry," Margo said. "Kiss me."

Cathy heard them kissing in the shadows. Was Larry really so shallow? She knew he wasn't that bright, but he had been an okay boyfriend until the band started. Jack was right, being in the group had gone to Larry's head. He was losing it.

"Larry, let's go to my room. We can sneak up the back way. My mother won't even hear us."

Don't do it! Cathy thought.

"Okay," Larry replied. "But let me get my bike."

"No," Margo told him. "It's now or never."

"Okay, let's go."

Cathy tore across the yard. She wanted to knock over Larry's bike, to trash it somehow. But then something else hit her, a way to get back at him. She would have to talk to the others, but she was sure they would go along. They all trusted Cathy's judgment.

When Larry showed up for the next rehearsal, he would have plenty of surprises to deal with!

Chapter 4

Todd's van rolled past Pelham Four Corners, heading for Wendy's place in Rocky Bank Estates. They were silent until the van stopped in front of her house, then they turned to look at each other at the same time. Their lips met for a kiss.

Todd broke away, laughing nervously. "Some rehearsal, huh?"

Wendy sighed. "Yeah. Larry's turned into a real jerk."

Todd slammed his fist in the palm of his hand. "I could've taken his stupid head off."

Wendy put her hand on his knee. "No, he's not worth it. You don't want to get into trouble again."

Todd leaned forward, resting against the steering wheel. "Maybe we should just bag it, look for another group."

"No!" Wendy said quickly.

He turned to her. "You want to stay in the band?"

Wendy gazed toward her house. "My family can use the extra money when we start playing."

"Oh. Your father still hasn't found a job?"

Wendy shook her head. "No. My mom's working, but it's not enough. This band could turn into a regular thing for me. I don't want to blow it."

Todd smiled. "Hey, have I told you you're the greatest?"

"Todd—"

"Well, you are."

"Thanks."

They kissed again, then Wendy climbed out of the van. Todd waved to her and drove off toward Gaspee Farms, his own neighborhood.

Wendy let out a deep sigh. What if the band fell apart? She would lose the extra income that her family needed. Playing gigs, even at junior high schools, was better than working at a burger joint for minimum wage.

When Todd's van was out of sight, she turned and walked toward her house. By the time she got to the door, she could already hear her mother and father fighting inside. Tears began to roll down Wendy's cheeks. They *had* to keep the band together!

Larry had been such a creep. He was a real problem. But what could she do about him?

After her third-period class, Cathy stood in the hallway, watching for Wendy. She was sure Wendy was on her side. But what would she think about Cathy's remedy for the ills of the group—namely, Larry Hart? If Wendy agreed with her, she would try her idea on the rest of the band.

Cathy flinched when she felt a hand on her

shoulder. She turned, expecting to see Larry, but instead, Jack Akers was smiling at her.

"Oh, hi," she said indifferently.

Jack removed his hand from her shoulder. "Hi, Cathy. I was wondering if you'd like to sit with me at lunch."

Cathy shook her head. "Uh, no, Jack. I'm waiting for Wendy."

"Hey, we could all eat together," he said.

The look on his face told her that Jack wanted to be more than friends. She was tempted. Jack was a nice guy, good-looking and well-built, but she knew another relationship could ruin the band.

"I'm sorry, Jack," Cathy said. "Maybe some other time."

"Cathy, I—"

"Oh look," she said, cutting him off. "There's Wendy now. See you later, Jack. Thanks for the invitation."

Cathy ran toward Wendy. Jack watched her for a moment, then started off down the hall. He was frustrated that Cathy hadn't come around yet. He would take his anger out on his teammates at wrestling practice.

Cathy caught up to Wendy and stopped her in the hall. "Hi."

"Hi," Wendy replied. "What's doing?"

"Have you got lunch now?" Cathy asked.

Wendy nodded. "Yeah."

"Let's go to the cafeteria," Cathy told her. "I have to talk to you."

47

"It's about the group, isn't it?"

"Yeah," Cathy replied.

They went through the lunch line and found a secluded table in the corner, but neither one of them touched their food. Cathy talked, and Wendy listened like a concerned friend.

Wendy thought Cathy made a lot of sense. There was only one way to go with the group. The girls were in complete agreement. And by the time the Saturday rehearsal arrived, they would have convinced the other members of the band to go along with their plan.

Margo pressed her thick red lips to Larry's mouth, kissing him. Larry wrapped his arms around her, drawing her close. She wasn't as smart or as talented as Cathy, but she had what he needed.

Margo broke off the kiss and looked into his eyes. "Wow, Larry, nobody has ever kissed me like that. You're really hot."

"Sure, Margo. Listen, I've got to go. I have rehearsal, and I'm already late. I'll see you tonight."

Margo stepped back, pouting a little. She wore a long white T-shirt that fell to her bare knees. Margo wasn't smart, but she was a lot of fun. They had been getting together in her room while her mother was at work. Larry was sure that Cathy knew about them, but so what. He always parked his Honda in front of Margo's house, right next door to Cathy's place.

"I want to come to rehearsal with you," Margo said.

Larry grimaced. "I don't think that's such a good idea."

"Why can't I?"

"Margo, I told you, we're going to have a gig soon. You ruin my concentration when you're around. You can come to the gig."

Margo folded her arms over her chest. "It's Cathy, isn't it? You're still hung up on her."

Larry frowned and shook his head. "No, Cathy and I are through."

A pain spread through his body. He felt bad about the way things had happened between him and Cathy. He had handled it poorly, but it was done.

Margo put her hands on his shoulders, leaning into him. "Maybe I could be in the group, Larry."

"What?"

"Yeah," she went on. "I could sing backup and play the tambourine. I'm good enough, I just know it."

Larry had to put her off. "Margo, I gotta split."

"Oh, please, Larry. Talk to them. The group will listen to you. If you say you want me in the band, they'll—"

"Maybe," he replied, just to get her to ease up. "But I can't promise you anything."

She kissed him again. "I love you so much. We'll be so happy when we're both in the group."

"Sure, Margo. I'll see you after rehearsal."

"I'll be waiting."

49

Larry left her room and headed out of the house. He had no intention of getting Margo into the group. He was going to say that the band didn't want her, that he had been outvoted by the others.

Outside, Larry walked down the alley between Margo's place and Cathy's. As he drew near the garage, he could hear the group already playing. He stopped dead when the thump of a bass drum reverberated in the crisp autumn air.

"What the—"

Larry broke into a run. He threw open the doors of the garage and stared into the light. The band immediately stopped playing. Larry's eyes widened at the sight of the new drummer, a young-looking kid with short black hair.

Larry wheeled toward Cathy, who stood behind her sound board. "What's going on here?"

Cathy smirked at him. "You've been replaced, Larry."

"Replaced?" He glared at the others. "What are you talking about? How could you replace me?"

No one would look him in the eye. The new drummer was the only one who glanced in his direction, but when he saw Larry's hostility, he quickly looked away.

Larry pointed at the black-haired kid. "Who's this geek?"

"His name is Paul Stark," Cathy replied.

She was trembling, even though the moment was something of a triumph. Emotions surged inside her. But she had to stay cool, to beat Larry at his own game.

"Man, this is bogus!" Larry cried. "You can't replace me with this dweeb."

Jack Akers took a step toward Larry. "He's not a dweeb, Hart. He's a pretty good drummer. And he was on time for rehearsal."

Larry pointed a finger at Jack. "Stay out of this, muscle-head!"

Jack tensed.

"No, Jack!" Cathy said. "Leave him alone. Larry, split. We've got a rehearsal in progress."

Larry stepped forward angrily. "You can't do this. Todd, Wendy . . ."

"You blew it, Hart," Todd said. "Paul is our drummer now. We voted on it."

"Wendy," Larry railed, "is this guy as good as me?"

Wendy looked at the floor. "He was on time, Larry. And he doesn't have an attitude. You asked for it."

In desperation, Larry grabbed Cathy's arm. "Come on, we're going to work this out."

Jack quickly unstrapped his bass guitar. "Lay off, Hart."

Larry tried to drag Cathy out of the garage. "I'm not finished."

"Let go of her!" Jack snarled.

Cathy managed to pull away. "Get out of here, Larry!"

"You jerks!" Larry cried. "You're the ones who blew it. You won't even last one gig without me."

Jack moved closer to Cathy, putting his arm around her shoulder. "We'll take our chances."

Larry had one last shot. "Darren, buddy—did you go along with this bogus vote?"

Darren nodded slightly. "Wendy's right, Larry. You had an attitude. And you were always late."

Larry pointed at the new drummer. "This geek isn't going to play my drums!" Larry started toward Paul.

Jack stepped in front of him. "They're not your drums, Hart. Your set is outside in boxes. We packed them up today."

"You muscleoid jerk!"

Larry drew back to take a swing at Jack, but Jack saw it coming a mile away. He ducked the blow and grabbed Larry, wrestling him to the ground.

Larry grunted and fought back, but he wasn't strong enough to take Jack. Jack pinned him to the floor of the garage and rubbed Larry's face in the dust.

"Let me up!" Larry snarled.

"Not until you promise to back off!"

"Let go of me!"

"Are you going to leave?" Jack demanded.

"You jerk!"

"Say you'll leave, Hart."

"All right, all right!"

Jack released his hold.

Larry jumped to his feet and glared at everyone. "You're going to regret this. All of you!"

Jack pointed toward the door. "Hit the pavement, Hart."

Larry shot a nasty look at Cathy. "I know you did this! You won't get away with it. Do you hear me?"

Cathy grinned smugly at her ex-boyfriend. "Bye, Larry. We're all going to miss you."

Larry stormed out, brushing past a young girl who was making her way into the garage. The girl watched him go by her, then turned to look at Cathy.

"Are you Cathy Malone?" the girl asked.

Cathy took a deep breath and nodded. "That's me."

"I'm Frieda Dietrich, from Lincoln Junior High. I've come to listen to your band. You know, for the dance."

"Sure," Cathy replied. "Just give us a minute."

"Great!" Frieda said. "Wow, you guys really know how to play. Bon Jovi and everything."

Cathy smiled. She was happy that the scene with Larry hadn't disturbed the sound of the group. Even with the new drummer, they didn't play badly. They were certainly good enough for seventh- and eighth-graders.

"So you want us for the gig?" Cathy asked.

Frieda nodded. "Sure, I'll tell the student council."

"Thanks," Cathy said. "We'll see you at the dance."

When Frieda was gone, Cathy turned to look at

the rest of the group. They were all smiling. They had their first gig!

Todd raised his fists in the air. "We did it!"

Wendy grabbed Todd and gave him a big kiss. "We're going to make it! That creep Larry can't hold us back."

Darren glanced toward the garage door. "He was really mad. I hope he doesn't come back."

Jack bristled. "If he does, I'll take his head off."

Cathy tried to be cheerful, even though she still had a bad taste in her mouth. "Hey, now that we have a gig, we need a name for the group. Any suggestions?"

Paul Stark listened as they considered a name for the band. He didn't offer his own ideas—he had just joined. He liked everyone and the sound was good, but after Larry's little show, Paul was wondering what he had gotten himself into.

"How about The Radicals?" Todd offered.

"There's a band with that name over in Porterville," Cathy replied.

"I've got it," Darren said. "Why don't we combine the names of our band members? You know, like Wilson Phillips."

"Not bad," Cathy said.

Paul raised his hand. "Hey, I don't think my name should be up there, since I just came into the group."

Cathy smiled at him. "Don't worry, Paul. You're here to stay. You sounded good tonight. In fact, Stark Steele wouldn't be a bad name for the group."

Jack shook his head. "Well, Jack Steele doesn't work. How about Darren's last name? Quick Steele."

"I kind of dig it," Wendy said. "It would be better than my name."

"We're getting closer," Cathy rejoined. "Hey, I've got it. Let's honor our former drummer."

"No way!" Jack said.

Cathy grinned—she had a way to pay back Larry. "No, it'll be great. Try this. Heart of Steel. We'll take the *e* from the end of Todd's last name and put it in Larry's. It's radical."

Wendy smiled. "Yeah. Heart of Steel. I like it. And we do a lot of heavy metal. It fits us."

"Won't that make Larry mad?" Paul asked cautiously. "I mean, he was pretty steamed."

"Who cares?" Wendy said. "Let's vote on it."

With some reassurances from Jack that he could handle Larry, they all voted to adopt the new name for the group.

Cathy had a wicked grin on her face. *Heart of Steel*. Whoever said revenge was sweet knew what he was talking about.

"They *what!*" Margo cried.

Larry threw his fist against the wall. "They bounced me out of the group!"

"They can't do that!"

Larry started to pace back and forth, unable to release the anger that burned inside him. "I hate them. I'm going to get them all!"

"This ruins everything," Margo said. "You

were the best one in that group. They won't be able to make it without you."

Larry stopped, glaring at her. "That's what I said. They're sunk in the water. Compared to me, they're a bunch of amateurs."

"It was Cathy," Margo said. "She can't stand it that you're seeing me now. She started it all."

"She's going to pay for this. Big time!"

Margo moved toward him, putting her hands on his shoulders. "You're the best, Larry. They're nothing without you."

Larry wanted to believe her. The members of the group had some nerve. Who did Jack think he was, pushing him around like that? They were all a bunch of losers. Larry would make them sorry that they ever threw him out of the group.

"I love you, Larry," Margo said. "And I'll help you. Together, we can show those creeps."

"I've got to think of something," Larry said. "It's got to be good. I'll take care of those jerks."

"Sure, honey. We can do it together."

Larry turned away from her. He walked toward the window of Margo's room, gazing toward the garage where the ax had fallen. Margo stepped up beside him. When Larry moved away, Margo stayed at the window. She saw Cathy and Jack coming out of the garage.

"Larry, look at this."

He came back to the window. "Those jerks. I'll bet they're talking about me."

"Look!"

Larry's eyes grew wide when he saw Jack put

his arms around Cathy. They started to kiss. Larry almost yanked the curtains away from the window.

"I'll kill them!" Larry cried. "I'll kill them all!"

Cathy was surprised when Jack tried to kiss her. She hesitated for a moment when their lips met, but then she had to pull away.

"Jack, please . . ."

He put his hands on her shoulders. "Cathy, I care about you. And I know you care about me."

"Jack, we just solved one problem with the band—"

"And we did the right thing," he said. "Hart was going to hold us back. But he's gone now, and you and I can be together."

Cathy looked into his kind blue eyes. He was nice, intelligent, protective, and handsome. But he just wasn't her type.

"Jack, the thing with Larry . . ."

Jack bristled. "He's not going to bother you while I'm here. He's history. I'll make sure he leaves us alone."

He tried to kiss her again. Cathy gently pushed him away. She knew it had been a mistake to let Jack stay after the others had left, but she had wanted him around in case Larry came back.

"I love you, Cathy. I love you more than Larry ever could. And you care about me. Don't you?"

"Jack, you're my friend. But I—I need more time. I can't jump into anything right now."

He sighed. "I understand, Cathy. I'll wait. You're going to love me, you'll see."

Gazing into his smiling face, she wished that she could love him. But the spark just wasn't there, and she couldn't force it.

"Good night, Jack."

"I'll walk you to your house."

They moved across the yard together. Jack was so sweet. He didn't try to kiss her good night. She resisted giving him a peck on the cheek, because it wasn't right to encourage him.

When Jack left, Cathy went upstairs to her room. Her heart was pounding and she had a sick feeling in her stomach. She should have been glad about the way they had handled the situation with Larry, but there was a horrible nagging in her gut.

Chapter 5

The Lincoln Junior High auditorium was jumping with the vibrant sounds of rock and roll. Heart of Steel cranked up the volume, thrilling the seventh- and eighth-graders who danced under the multicolored lights. They were having a wild time. For many of the kids, it was the first time they had heard a live rock group.

Cathy sat at her control board, tapping her feet to the heavy rhythms of her band. She kept her eyes on the readout monitors, making sure the sound levels stayed balanced. She had also rigged the colored lights that flashed on the high stage platform, which made the group look really big-time.

Watching Heart of Steel filled Cathy with a sense of satisfaction. Some of the early unpleasantness with Larry still lingered in her thoughts, but she tried hard to put it behind her. It was a great accomplishment to have her first rock group playing a gig. Even without Larry, the group sounded tight.

On stage, Todd Steele was a maniac. He played well to the audience, leaping around, making monster faces, shaking his long hair, jerking and swaying as if he had been performing for years. His wailing lead guitar seemed to have a life of its own.

Jack Akers was more laid back under the lights. His bass was on time, but he wasn't animated like Todd. He was content just to play his thumping rhythms.

The biggest surprise had been Darren Quick. In rehearsal he had struggled to get the songs right, but something about the audience caused the performer in him to awaken. His fingers flew over the keyboard with precision. He bobbed his head, and his body shook with the primal beat. And his new, cooler clothes really made him look different.

Wendy was in heaven. She moved like a rock-and-roll diva under the lights, handling each song with a professional demeanor that couldn't be learned. She put her heart into her performance, thinking about getting paid later on. Bigger and better things would happen for the group—she just knew it.

On drums, Paul Stark was definitely the weakest member of the band. Cathy had to admit that Paul wasn't as good as Larry. But Paul could carry a beat, and he didn't hurt the group. Cathy was sure he'd get better with time.

When the band finished the first set, they struck a pose and Cathy brought down the lights for a moment. Cheers and applause rose from the junior-high kids. When Cathy turned on the lights again, Jack kicked off the bass run for the "break" song.

Wendy leaned in toward the microphone. "Put your hands together, Lincoln!"

The kids cheered loudly.

Wendy flashed them an appreciative smile. "Thanks. We're going to take a little break now—"

A collective groan rolled through the crowd. "No!"

"More, more!"

"Don't stop playing!"

Wendy laughed a little. "Take it easy. We'll be back in fifteen minutes. In the meantime, you boys and girls take a break yourselves. When we come back, we're going to rock this house down!"

Todd leaped forward, burning a couple of hot riffs and mugging at the kids.

"Yeah!"

"Heart of Steel rules!"

"Steel's number one!"

The music died, and Cathy brought down the lights. Applause and cheers continued for a few minutes, until the kids realized the first set was over. From her position backstage, Cathy watched as the band members made their way into the wings.

Jack ran toward her. "How'd we sound?"

Cathy nodded. "Good!"

She thought there were a few rough spots, but she didn't want to upset them now. They could work it out. Paul needed the most practice.

Todd raised a fist in the air. "Did you see those little mutants? They were eating us up."

Wendy smirked at him. "Down, boy. We don't want any more ego trips."

Darren was smiling. "This is great. I never knew that playing in front of a crowd was like this."

Paul was the only one who didn't seem confident. "Man, I stunk. I'm sorry, guys, I—"

"You didn't stink," Cathy said quickly. "Just relax, Paul. Go with it. You sounded fine."

Jack slipped up next to Cathy, giving her a hopeful smile. "How's it going, love?"

Cathy tried to smile, even though she felt uncomfortable around Jack. She would never be able to return his feelings. She didn't want to hurt him, because he had been so sweet.

"You sound good," Cathy told him. "It's a great gig."

"We couldn't do it without you," Jack replied. "You made it all happen."

Cathy gave him a playful push. "Get something to drink. We're back on in fifteen minutes."

They all grabbed sodas and juice from a cooler backstage. Cathy watched the clock. Professional groups played forty-five-minute sets. She didn't want to disappoint their audience, even if they were only twelve and thirteen years old.

She finally clapped her hands together. "Okay, back to work."

But when they turned toward the stage platform, they froze.

An angry scowl spread over Jack's face. "Oh, no. I don't believe it!"

Darren's mouth fell open. "Where did he come from?"

"He's got some nerve coming here," Wendy said.

Todd shook his head. "He can't be for real."

Cathy's eyes had grown wide. Larry Hart had arrived backstage and was stomping toward them with a wicked look on his face.

Paul's face had turned white. "I'm in trouble now."

"Let me handle it," Cathy said.

Larry walked up to Paul and held out his hand. "Give me those sticks," he said angrily. "Give them to me right now."

Cathy stepped in front of Paul. "Get lost, Larry. You're not in this group anymore. Or did you forget?"

Larry made a threatening move toward Paul and Cathy.

Jack was right there. He grabbed Larry and spun him around, pushing him backward.

"You heard her," Jack said. "Get lost."

Larry smiled and gestured behind him. "I'm ready for you, muscle-boy. I brought a couple of my friends to back me up. If you try to stop me, they'll fix you good."

Jack glanced over Larry's shoulder. Two large guys in leather jackets lurked in the wings. One of them pointed at Jack.

"Is that how it stands, Hart?" Jack asked.

Larry glared at Cathy, ignoring Jack. "Pretty cute, huh. Calling yourselves Heart of Steel." He turned to Paul. "I mean it. Give me those drumsticks."

Paul backed away. "This isn't right, Larry."

Larry took another step toward Paul. Jack grabbed him by the front of his leather vest and they stood eye to eye.

"I don't care if you did bring your goons," Jack said. "You're not coming in here and trashing our gig."

"Have it your way," Larry replied. "But when I give the word, my boys are going to wreck this place."

Cathy put her hand on Jack's shoulder. "Let him go."

"He's mine!" Jack growled.

"No," Cathy replied. "If things get out of hand, we won't get paid. And we'll have a reputation as a trouble band."

"We don't need that," Wendy said. "Maybe we should let him play."

Jack let go of Larry. "You're a jerk, Hart."

Larry snatched the drumsticks away from Paul. "I'm the drummer now."

Todd stepped up beside Jack. "Forget it. We can take these clowns."

"No!" Cathy said. "Let Larry play the next set. Paul can come back after that."

Larry shook his head. "No way. I play the whole gig or we tear this place apart. Take it or leave it."

Jack shook his fist at Larry. "You're a real butt-head, Hart. I'm not going to let you get away with this."

Wendy didn't want trouble either. "Easy, Jack. Let him play. It's the only way out of this. I'm sorry, Paul, but the show has to go on. We'll get it all settled later. But right now, we've got to protect our job and our reputation."

"Smart move, Wendy," Larry said. "If you ever want to ditch Steele, you know where to find me."

"Don't hold your breath," Wendy replied.

Larry turned away, walking toward his brawny friends. Margo was with them. She threw her arms around Larry's neck and kissed him.

Cathy clenched her fist and banged it on the wall. "That cretin!"

"He's going to ruin us," Wendy said.

"Not if I can help it," Cathy replied.

"What can we do?" Jack asked.

Cathy told the others to stay backstage and then quickly took Wendy aside. "Stall him for a minute," she whispered.

Wendy frowned. "What are you going to do?"

"I'm going to fix Mr. Hart once and for all," Cathy replied. "But you have to get him back here and keep him busy."

"Why?"

"Just do it. And tell Paul to be ready."

"Okay, okay."

Wendy looked across the stage, smiling at Larry. She urged him to come over to see her.

Larry ran through the shadows. Margo and the goons disappeared backstage.

When Larry was talking to Wendy, Cathy hurried to her sound board. As she moved in the shadows, she could hear Jack, Paul, and Todd arguing among themselves. They were nodding at Larry, flashing grim looks of determination.

Cathy threw the switch that shut off the lights to the backstage area. She found her way onto the drummer's platform, and began to loosen every nut and bolt on the drum set. Larry was going to bomb. The drum set was on a high platform, so everyone would get a good view of Larry making a fool of himself. Maybe then he would leave them alone.

Cathy stepped down and went back to her sound board. "Okay," she said to Wendy. "Make sure you announce that we have a new drummer for the rest of the gig. I'll put a special spotlight on you, Larry."

Larry smirked at her. "Smart girl. Now these j-high geeks will get to hear what a real drummer sounds like."

Jack shook his head. "When this is over, Hart, it's you and me on the bus to fist city!"

Larry waved the drumsticks at him. "Just keep the beat going, Akers. And don't get in my way if I decide to do a drum solo."

"Places," Cathy said.

The band took the stage again. The curtain went up. Cathy hit the lights, and the kids cheered wildly.

Wendy reluctantly stepped up to the microphone. "Uh, we have someone joining us on drums for the rest of the night. His name is Larry Hart."

The spotlight flashed on, bathing Larry in bright light atop the high platform. He raised his drumsticks over his head and brought them down with a crash. But as soon as his foot thumped the bass pedal, the drum set started to fall apart.

Larry froze with a dull expression on his face. He tried to hit the cymbals, but they came flying off their stands. The tomtoms rolled onto the stage, landing at Jack's feet.

"Rock and roll!" Jack cried with a wild laugh.

Cathy grinned triumphantly, keeping the spotlight on Larry. He tried to jump off the platform, but he tripped and tumbled into the bass drum. The junior-high kids began to laugh at him. They thought it was a joke, part of the act.

Larry began to swear. He tried to regain his balance, but his feet got caught in the wrecked hardware and he fell backward.

Margo rushed from the wings and helped him down. Together, they staggered off into the night. Larry had been justly humiliated.

Cathy's prank had worked! All they had to do was reassemble the drum set and they could play again. She called Paul to come out of the dressing room.

"Awesome," Paul said, smiling.

"Get it back together," Cathy said. "Larry's history."

As Paul moved away, Cathy saw Wendy coming toward her. Wendy didn't look happy.

"How could you do that?" Wendy said. "It's not professional. It makes us look like a bunch of babies."

"Relax," Cathy said. "Larry's the only one who looked like a jerk. We can claim it was part of the show."

"What if we don't get paid?" Wendy challenged. "I need this money, Cathy. You shouldn't fight your private battles at the expense of the band. It's going to ruin our reputation. No one will want us to play."

"I did it for *all* of us," Cathy replied. "Listen. They still love us."

The cheers for Steel were rising out of the crowd. The junior-high kids pushed against the front of the stage, reaching for the band.

The anger faded from Wendy's beautiful face. "Wow. They really do love us. Cathy, I—I'm sorry."

Cathy winked at her. "Don't worry, Wendy. We're hot."

Wendy smiled. "I guess you know what you're doing."

"As soon as Paul is ready, let's rock," Cathy said.

Wendy moved back onto the stage.

Cathy felt triumphant behind her sound board. Paul put the drums together and climbed onto the platform. Wendy kicked off a song, and they were into the second set again. The crowd was more wild than before.

During the next break, everyone kept an eye out for Larry and his goons, but they didn't come back. The third set was going to start without a hitch.

"Break's over," Cathy said. "Back to work."

The kids went wild when Steel came back onto the stage. They cheered for Paul as he climbed back onto the platform. But when he sat down, there was a cracking sound. Everyone's head turned in slow motion.

The cracking noise turned into a rumble. Cathy's eyes grew wide with horror. The whole drummer's platform had begun to collapse!

The drummer's platform seemed to implode, giving way in the center. Paul cried out as he disappeared in a heap of wood and metal. At first, the junior-high kids thought it was another joke, but then the members of the band began to shout for help and the crowd realized that this time it was for real. Cries of fear and disbelief rose in the audience as the kids began to panic.

Wendy grabbed the microphone. "Everyone, please, stay calm!"

Cathy and the other band members rushed to help Paul. They could hear him moaning at the bottom of the pile. His body was twisted and broken. Some of the rubble had fallen on top of him.

"We've got to get him out of there!" Cathy cried.

Wendy screamed into the microphone. "Somebody call an ambulance!"

Confusion filled the auditorium as students and teachers rushed back and forth.

"Help me!" Cathy called to the guys.

Jack, Todd, and Darren began to tear at the wreckage, trying to clear it away from Paul's body. As they worked, the moaning from beneath the pile suddenly stopped.

"He's dead!" someone cried from the audience.

"No!" Cathy said. "Get him out of there."

Paul was wedged between two rectangles of the fallen stage. Jack strained, trying to pull away one of the sections, but it was too heavy.

The others leaned in to help him. They grunted and broke a sweat with the effort. The section finally began to move.

When it was clear, Paul's body rolled over and his pale face gaped up at them. His eyes were turned back into his head so only the whites were visible.

"My God," Cathy said under her breath.

She stared at Paul's body. For a moment, she thought he had died. Then his chest rose and fell slowly.

"Look at his leg!" Darren cried.

Paul's leg was shattered. The bone had pushed through the skin, and red blood ran over the white shard, gushing from the hole in Paul's shin.

* * *

The emergency room of Cresswell Community Hospital had a medicinal smell that made Cathy gag. She had followed the ambulance to the hospital, and now she sat on the plastic bench in the waiting room. The other members of the group had stayed behind to clean up the mess.

It was a horrible way to end their first gig. Cathy felt an overwhelming pang of guilt. It was all her fault. She had never meant for Paul to be hurt. The reputation of the band was ruined. They wouldn't even be paid for the gig.

"Miss Malone?"

Cathy looked up to see a young woman doctor standing in front of her. "Yes, I'm Cathy Malone."

"Are you a friend of Paul Stark?"

Cathy nodded. "Yes, is he all right?"

The doctor sat down next to her. "He's doing better. His leg was fractured in three places. I'm afraid he'll need an operation—the bone will need steel pins to hold it together while it heals properly. He's going to be fine, but he'll have to stay in the hospital for a while."

"I want to see him," Cathy said.

"I don't think it's a good time," the doctor replied. "His parents are with him now, and he'll be going into surgery any minute."

Cathy nodded. "I understand. Thank you for telling me."

The doctor got up and walked down the white corridor.

Cathy leaned back in the chair. Everything had been fine until she had sabotaged the drum set. But why did the platform collapse? Surely the falling drums couldn't have caused the accident. Paul had crashed *after* the drum set was reassembled. Had someone tampered with the platform between the second and third sets?

An idea suddenly came to Cathy, and she frowned. "Larry!"

Cathy got up, heading for the exit. As she went through the emergency-room doors, she felt a hand on her shoulder. Startled, Cathy spun her head to look. Jack Akers was looming over her.

"Jack, what are you . . ."

He pointed toward the parking lot. "Todd and the others are out in the van. How's Paul?"

"He's going to be all right."

Jack put his arms around her. "How are you?"

Cathy backed away from the embrace. "I feel horrible. Come on, I'll tell the others."

As they walked to the van, Cathy wondered if Jack could have done something to the platform. After all, he didn't like Larry. Maybe he had trashed the platform so Larry would take the fall, only to have Paul become the victim.

"How is he?" Todd asked as they climbed into the van.

"He's going to live," Cathy replied.

Wendy exhaled a breath of relief. "Thank God!"

"They're going to operate on his leg," Cathy said.

Darren grimaced. "An operation?"

Cathy nodded sadly. "They have to put it back together with pins."

Jack shuddered. "Man, I wonder why that platform collapsed?"

A shiver played across Cathy's shoulders. "Just take me home."

Jack looked longingly at her. "If you're cold, Cathy, you can have my jacket. You want it?"

She shook her head. "No, just take me home."

Todd put the van into gear and started for the Upper Basin. They were quiet as they rolled toward Cathy's place.

When they turned a dark corner, Cathy leaned forward, squinting into the shadows. "Oh, no!"

A sheriff's patrol car sat in the driveway of Cathy's house. More trouble. Just what the band needed.

Sheriff Tommy Hagen was a big, ruddy man with a penetrating stare. He glared right through Cathy, making her feel guilty. She was sitting in her living room with her mother and the rest of the band.

"You're Cathy Malone?" the sheriff asked.

She nodded. "Yes, sir." Her heart was pounding. Cathy had never liked cops.

Hagen kept his steely gaze focused on her. "You want to tell me what happened tonight at the junior high?"

Cathy shrugged. "The platform collapsed. Our drummer was hurt."

"It just collapsed?"

73

"Yes, sir. That's right."

Jack started to say something, but the sheriff stopped him. "I want to hear it from Miss Malone. Who set up the platform in the first place?"

"We all did," Cathy replied. "We had to do it before the gig."

"Where did you get the platform?"

"It belongs to the junior high. The maintenance people were supposed to set it up, but when we got there, it wasn't ready. We had to do it ourselves."

The sheriff's accusing eyes looked at some notes and then lifted again, narrowing at Cathy. "My deputies studied that pile of wreckage, young lady. There seemed to be some things missing from the platform structure."

Cathy frowned back at him. "Missing?"

"Two bolts," the sheriff said. "Key bolts that hold the platform together. Someone had taken them away. That's what caused the platform to collapse."

"That's impossible," Cathy said. "I checked that platform before Paul set up his drums. Everything was in place."

"You're sure?" Hagen asked skeptically.

Cathy nodded weakly. "I checked it myself."

Hagen shook his head. "My men are experts. They say the platform wouldn't have fallen if those bolts had been there."

Damn! Cathy thought. Someone *had* sabotaged the platform. But who?

Hagen kept his eyes on her. "Some of the witnesses say there was more trouble at the dance tonight."

Cathy stiffened. "Like what?"

"Maybe you should tell me," Hagen replied.

Cathy looked away. "It was personal. We had a guy in the band, but we had to fire him. He showed up wanting to play. So we let him, because he threatened to make a scene. His name is Larry Hart. You should talk to him."

"We already have," Hagen replied. "He says you did something to the drum set to make it fall apart. Is that right, Cathy?"

She looked up, meeting Hagen's gaze. "Yes. I loosened some of the heads and cymbals."

"Why?"

"I—I didn't want him at the gig. None of us did. But we had to let him play, because he brought some goons with him. He threatened to trash the gig if we didn't let him go on. I just wanted to embarrass him so he'd leave us alone."

Hagen glanced at the others. "Is that right? This Larry barged in on you?"

Jack grunted. "Yeah. He's been causing trouble all along."

"He did have goons with him," Darren rejoined.

Todd just nodded, keeping quiet. He was afraid the sheriff would recognize him.

Wendy sighed. "It's a shame Larry had to cause a scene. He's really a good drummer."

Hagen focused on Cathy again. "So, maybe

while you were trashing the drums, you slipped down and took those bolts out of the platform."

Cathy's mother stood up. "I will not sit in my own house and listen to such accusations, Sheriff!"

"No, Mom," Cathy said. "It's all right. I swear. I never did anything to that platform."

"She's right," Wendy said. "I watched her from the wings while she fixed the drums for Larry. Cathy never went under the platform."

Hagen grimaced, shaking his head. "Well, kids, this doesn't look good for someone. You had trouble with this Larry, so that gives you motive to want to hurt him. You could all be covering for each other. I don't have anything on you, but I'm going to be watching you. Anybody who comes forward now can save a lot of trouble and maybe get a break in the end. How about it?"

But no one had anything to say.

Sheriff Hagen put on his hat. "Stay in touch, kids. I know I will." He left the house without looking back.

Cathy's mother let out a deep sigh. "What a rude man!"

The Heart of Steel members were all silent for a moment.

"We better call it a night," Cathy said.

The others agreed. An awkward silence hung in the air before they left.

Who had taken the key bolts from the drummer's platform? One of them? Their suspicions were a horrible punctuation mark to an already haunting night. And the bad feeling wouldn't go away for a long time, even after Heart of Steel began to play again.

Chapter 6

Paul Stark lay back in his hospital bed. "So," he said with a half-smile on his pale face. "Guess it'll be a while before I can work the bass pedal again. You guys'll have to find a new drummer."

The somber members of Heart of Steel were gathered around Paul's bed for Wednesday-night visiting hours. It was the first time the group had been together since Saturday, and everyone was uneasy. The group and the accident were the talk of Cresswell High. Dealing with the notoriety had been difficult—they were almost local celebrities of a dark sort.

Cathy smiled warmly at Paul. "How are you feeling, Starky?"

Paul sighed, running his hand along the plaster leg cast that hung from traction wires. "I'm okay. It hurts sometimes. But I'll be able to get out of bed tomorrow. They've got this solarium on the roof, a high-class gym for physical therapy. It'll be better than lying here all day."

"You look good," Wendy offered cheerfully.

Paul winked playfully at her. "You're a fox yourself, Wendy."

Todd smiled easily. "Hey, watch it, Paul. She's my girl, you know."

"Not if I can steal her," Paul replied.

Jack laughed. "Aw, he can't be in that bad a shape if he's picking up on the women." He turned and winked at Cathy. Cathy smiled weakly and looked away.

Darren squinted dubiously at Paul. "How was the operation?"

Paul shrugged. "I don't know. I was out cold. Hey, why don't you guys sign my cast? Cathy, you go first." He held up a black felt-tipped marker.

Cathy took the marker and signed his cast. "You better get well in a hurry."

Paul looked into Cathy's blue eyes. "Are you guys practicing yet?"

Cathy hesitated. "Uh, not really."

"Don't let this accident stop you," Paul replied. "You have to get another drummer and go on with the group."

Cathy couldn't tell him that the collapsing platform might not have been an accident. Paul had enough trouble dealing with his recovery. The other members of the group were as reticent as Cathy. They hadn't said a word about the band continuing, except for Wendy. She still really wanted the band to keep playing.

"You're a celebrity at Cresswell, Paul," Wendy said as she signed his cast. "The entertainment editor of the *Sentinel* interviewed me about the accident. Everyone's talking about you. It's the rage at school. Now everybody knows who we are. Heart of Steel is almost a household name."

"Really?" Paul said. "Wow, you guys can't give up now."

Wendy patted his hand. "We won't, Paul. Will we, guys?"

But there didn't seem to be any enthusiasm from the others.

Cathy shifted nervously on her feet. "We better go. It's getting late, and Paul has to rest so he can play with Steel again."

Paul sighed. "You guys come back soon. I'm going to be here for a couple of weeks."

Cathy touched his arm. "You won't be able to keep us away."

They filed out of Paul's room. When they were in the hall, Cathy stopped and the band members formed a semicircle around her.

"Okay," Cathy said, "I'll say it for all of us. Things are tense. We're all wondering about that platform. I want to be the first one to say that I didn't do anything to make it fall."

"Me neither," Wendy said quickly.

The others also denied having any part of it.

Jack put his hands on his hips. "If none of us did it, then who did?"

Cathy suddenly looked over Jack's shoulder. "This could be our answer right here."

They all turned to see Larry Hart striding down the hall, hand in hand with Margo Reardon.

Jack put his arm loosely around Cathy's shoulder. "Hart has got some nerve coming here."

As Larry came toward them, he leaned over and whispered something to Margo. Margo laughed a little.

"Well, well," Larry said, stopping in front of Cathy and the others. "Look what the cat dragged in."

Jack pointed a finger in Larry's face. "You're asking for it, creep."

"Me? What did I do?" Larry said innocently.

Cathy's eyes narrowed. "You did something to that platform to make it collapse, Larry. Admit it!"

Larry scowled at her. "Hey, I was up there, too. It could have fallen with me on it. I didn't do anything to that platform. You were the one who trashed the drums, Cathy. You were out to get *me*. You fixed it so I'd take the fall."

Jack cocked his arm back to take a swing at Larry, but Cathy stopped him.

"No, not here. Not in the hospital. Let's split."

She took Jack's arm, like they were together. She wanted Larry to be jealous. The group moved toward the elevator.

Jack glared back at Larry. "That jerk. He should have been the one who got hurt!"

Cathy drew away from Jack, looking up at him with quick surprise. What did he mean by that?

The elevator opened. At the other end of the hall, Larry watched them get into it. His face was bright red.

"Come on," Margo said. "Let's go talk to Paul." He didn't seem to hear her. "Larry . . ."

"Those geeks," Larry muttered. "I hate them. As far as I'm concerned, I wish they were all dead!"

Cathy sat in the back of Todd's van, looking out at the dark streets of Cresswell. Everyone was quiet.

Cathy sighed and looked down at her hands in her lap. Jack was sitting next to her. She had her doubts about Jack now. Had he taken the bolts so Larry would get hurt? She had been so sure that Larry was the culprit—but now she just didn't know.

Cathy wanted to talk to the band. They had to have an official meeting sooner or later to discuss the fate of the band, but she wasn't sure the time was right.

Todd guided the van into the driveway of Cathy's house. "Home sweet home, Cathy. We're here."

Cathy absently climbed out of the van and stood next to the passenger window where Wendy was sitting.

Wendy looked concerned. "Are you all right, Cathy?"

Cathy nodded, thinking that Wendy was the one member of the band that she really trusted. "I'm okay. I—I think we need to get together soon."

Wendy smiled a little. "Yeah. We have to line up another gig. The sooner the better, while we're still front-page news. We . . . we can't let this thing stop us."

"She's right," Jack called from the back of the van. "We've got to talk."

Todd leaned over, looking at Cathy. "How about Saturday?"

"Sure," Cathy replied. "My garage. The usual time?"

Everybody agreed. Todd backed the van out of the driveway. Cathy watched them disappear down the street. Except for Wendy, she wasn't sure that she knew who they really were.

As she walked up the front steps, Cathy had a bad feeling. She didn't have much hope. If she had been a gambler, Cathy would have wagered that Heart of Steel was finished.

It was a bet she would have lost.

Paul Stark was glad to see Thursday afternoon roll around, when he was scheduled for the beginning of his physical therapy. He wouldn't be working on the broken leg, but he'd get to exercise his upper body. Even if he was in a wheelchair, it would be better than lying in bed all day.

The therapist wheeled him up to the fifth-floor rooftop of the hospital. Paul felt the warmth of the afternoon sun in the solarium. He could see all of Cresswell through the bright, glass-walled windows. After an hour, Paul asked the therapist to let him stay. Evening shadows were falling on Cresswell, and Paul thought it would be nice to sit on the roof and watch the city as it grew dark. Finally, the therapist agreed.

She wheeled him to the edge of a ramp that led down to another exercise area. Paul sat there with his leg propped up, looking at Cresswell High in the distance. He wondered about his friends and the other members of the band. Paul hoped they would keep the band together so he could play again after he got out of the hospital.

"Paul," the therapist called, "I'm going down to the fourth floor for a moment to coordinate the next group of patients. Will you be all right?"

Paul just nodded, keeping his eyes on the glowing city beneath him. For a moment, he thought about going down the ramp to the exercise area below, but something stopped him.

Paul had always been a little afraid of heights. He didn't want to deal with the ramp by himself —he could see the glass wall at the bottom of the incline. Five stories was quite a drop if the wheelchair got away from him.

He sighed, wishing that his leg would stop hurting. The doctors told him that he would be able to walk again when it healed, but he was worried that he might be in pain for the rest of his life.

Suddenly, Paul felt a hand on his shoulder and jumped. He glanced back to see a familiar face looking down at him.

"Hi," Paul said. "What are you doing here?"

The person only smiled eerily. Suddenly, Paul

felt his wheelchair being shoved forward with a hard jerk.

"What are you doing? Hey! Wait! No—stop! Oh, my God!"

He tried to fight, but his fingers snapped in the spokes of the wheels. The chair rushed down the incline, barreling toward the glass wall at the end of the ramp.

The wall might have stopped him if his cast hadn't been elevated. It acted like a battering ram, breaking through the glass, shattering the huge panel. Paul shot through the jagged opening, screaming. He flipped out of the chair, tumbled over the safety rail, and fell in horrible slow motion toward the parking lot below.

As his screams echoed through the still evening air, the sidewalk rushed up to meet the terrified expression on his face. He hit the ground with tons of force.

His neck snapped as soon as he hit, making his death painless. He didn't feel all the bones breaking in his body. But the dull, meaty thud of his landing was heard on every floor of the hospital.

It didn't take long for a crowd to gather over the twisted body of the dead boy. It had obviously been an accident. No one noticed the killer who slipped out of the building, walking quickly past them, never turning to view the final result.

On Saturday, the group gathered in Cathy's garage. Paul's funeral had been a somber affair. No one in the band could believe what had happened. Was bad luck doomed to follow Heart of Steel? It made Cathy's news all the more macabre.

Todd sighed as he eased onto a wooden stool. "Major grief."

Wendy put her hand on his shoulder. "There was nothing we could do."

Cathy sat down behind her sound board. "Maybe this isn't the right time, but I think we should talk about the future of the band."

"What band?" Jack said with a cynical laugh. "We don't have any band."

Cathy looked at the others. "Do you feel the same way?"

Darren shook his head slowly. He had been getting a lot of attention at school from the girls who had once called him a wimp. Being in the group had made him famous. He liked playing rock and roll.

And Todd was really into being lead guitar for the band. His delinquent days were behind him now. He was on his way up, even though he was sad for Paul.

As for Jack—well, the band had given him a chance to get next to Cathy. That was what he wanted. He knew she would love him sooner or later.

Wendy voiced what the others were thinking. "It's really terrible about Paul," she said. "But we have to keep it together. We're just getting started. We could go places. And I need a job. I know we didn't get paid for the j-high gig, but there'll be other gigs down the road. And we're good, guys. Admit it."

Todd smiled and nodded. "We did rock the house down before Paul fell through that platform."

Cathy took a deep breath. "We have to vote on whether or not we want to continue with Heart of Steel, but first hear what I have to say. This is going to sound strange, but Wendy's right. We're more popular than ever. I've been getting offers for all kinds of gigs."

Wendy grinned. "Really?"

Cathy nodded. "Yes. Since Paul—I mean, well, I've had five calls from people who want us to play."

Jack was amazed. "Get out of town."

"I know it's weird," Cathy replied, "but all of a sudden we're the hottest high-school band in Cresswell."

"They want us," Wendy said. "This is great, guys. We were in the paper and on television. Publicity, even if it's bad, can bring gigs out of the woodwork. We're going to be famous!"

Todd looked at Cathy. "What kind of gigs?" he asked.

"Three junior high schools," Cathy replied. "But we've also had an offer from the Battle of the Bands next month at the Bridgewater Pavilion. I got the call this morning."

Wendy clapped her hands together. "Battle of the Bands at the Pavilion! Man, that's big time. Talent scouts come up from New York. Record people and managers see the show. We've made it, guys!"

Darren frowned. "Are we really that good? I mean, they may just want to see us because one of our guys was killed. People can have a morbid sense of curiosity."

"Yeah," Jack said, "like who's going to die next."

"Who cares *why* they want us?" Wendy said. "They want us!"

"We also have an offer for the Halloween dance at Cresswell High," Cathy went on. "The president of the student council asked me himself."

Darren shook his head. "Why do we have to get hot now, after what happened to Paul?"

Wendy put her hand on his shoulder. "Bittersweet Darren. Sometimes that's how it happens, good and bad at the same time. But we can't ignore the good things. This is our chance."

"Well, good or bad, we're in demand," Cathy said. "I feel sort of creepy, but we have to vote on whether or not we're going to continue. I have to give people answers."

They looked at each other. Regardless of what had happened, they all had their reasons for wanting to continue.

"I vote no," Todd said suddenly.

Wendy glared at him. "What?"

"For the junior-high gigs," he said. "But I vote yes for the Halloween dance and the Battle of the Bands."

"Great!" Wendy said, smiling again. "I vote yes, too. Come on, guys. We can't let it die now."

Darren lowered his head. "I'm sorry about Paul, but this is what we've been working for. We can't turn it down. I vote yes."

Jack smiled at Cathy. "I vote yes. What about you, Cathy?"

Cathy hesitated. Her dream had come true. She had her own popular rock band, but she had never anticipated that fame would bring such mixed emotions. Everyone wanted to see them because of the bizarre events that had surrounded the band, but how could she turn down the chance to play the decent gigs they had been waiting for?

"Cathy?" Jack asked again.

She nodded. "Okay, I vote yes. We keep the band alive."

Wendy let out a happy cry and hugged Cathy. "Yes! We can do it, guys. I know we can."

"One more thing," Cathy insisted. "We dedicate the gigs to Paul."

Everyone agreed. They wouldn't forget Paul. His memory would be kept alive in their music.

"The Pavilion!" Wendy said dreamily. "The biggest local rock gig of the year. First prize at the Battle of the Bands is five thousand dollars!"

"We're going to need a drummer," Cathy said. "Any suggestions?"

"Let's hold auditions again," Wendy replied enthusiastically.

Cathy's brow fretted. "Sure. Anyone brave

enough to try out for this band gets the job. We haven't had much luck with drummers so far."

"No problem," Wendy replied. "When word gets out that we're looking for a drummer, they'll beat down the door!"

Wendy was right. Cathy didn't even have to make an official announcement about the vacancy in Heart of Steel. All week long, her phone had been ringing off the hook. She turned down anyone who didn't have previous experience in a band.

By the next Saturday, she had narrowed down the candidates to five. Todd borrowed a set of drums from a friend of his, a girl named Felicia Hale, who was also one of the auditioners. Felicia had asked if she could play last, and Cathy had agreed.

Cathy felt strange when the band assembled for the first time since Paul's death, but the other members of the group didn't seem awkward at all. They were upbeat, ready to play again.

"Looking good, Cathy," Jack said with a wink.

She ignored him and started to set levels on her sound board. When they were in tune, the first drummer took his place behind the group and they kicked off into a heavy-metal number.

Cathy didn't have to hear much to determine that the drummer wasn't good enough. She dismissed him and called in the next hopeful. She was disappointed again and again, until Todd's friend Felicia took stage with the group.

From the first rap on the snare, Cathy knew that Felicia was good. She studied Felicia as she played. The tall, skinny, blond girl looked pretty under the light, almost as striking as Wendy. Felicia had a delicate quality that hardened as soon as she picked up the drumsticks. The group made it through the entire number with Felicia following perfectly.

Cathy applauded when they were finished. "Great! I don't know about you guys, but I think Felicia is our drummer."

Jack nodded to Cathy. "I'll trust your judgment. If Cathy wants her, she's in."

Darren shrugged. "Sounded good to me."

Todd grinned. "Yeah! I knew you could do it, babe."

Wendy was frowning. She hadn't known that Todd and Felicia were friends. For the first time, Wendy had competition on stage. She moved over next to Todd, taking his arm.

"What do you think, Wendo?" Todd asked. "Isn't she great?"

"Yes," Wendy said dryly. "Great. I just hope she can learn all of the songs before Halloween."

Felicia smiled at Wendy. "I'm a quick study. Just give me a list of songs and turn me loose."

"Welcome to the band," Cathy said. *Maybe the bad times are all behind us,* she thought.

Heart of Steel had a new drummer. But they wouldn't have her for long.

Chapter 7

Wendy Coles sat alone in the cafeteria at Cresswell High. As she nibbled at her lunch, she could hear the girls at the table behind her, gossiping about Heart of Steel and the Halloween dance.

"That's the lead singer!"

"She's so pretty."

"Hey, did you hear about that guy getting killed? Wild."

"I wonder who's going to get it this time?"

"Oh, don't be so gross!"

"No, it's exciting. Everyone will be there. I can't wait to see what happens. It's going to be radical."

Wendy pushed away her lunch tray and smiled to herself. The group's popularity had soared since Paul's accident. They were really on their way straight to the top. After the Halloween dance, everyone would want to hire them.

"I wouldn't miss this dance for anything."

"What kind of costume are you going to wear?"

"I thought I'd come as a dead drummer!"

"Oh, you're so gross."

Wendy leaned back, fantasizing about the big

break that would come after the Pavilion gig. A record executive would see her and offer the band a contract. Or maybe they would offer her a solo contract. She could be the next Madonna.

A stadium full of people cheered and chanted her name. Movie offers followed. With Cresswell a memory, her family moved into a mansion in Los Angeles. Her father drove a Mercedes and her mother shopped on Rodeo Drive. The tabloids linked her name with a handsome film star.

"Wendy?"

Her trance broken, Wendy looked up to see Felicia standing in front of her, holding a lunch tray.

"Mind if I sit down?" Felicia asked.

Wendy shrugged. "No, go ahead."

Felicia sat on the other side of the table, peering at Wendy. "Listen, I want your honest opinion. How am I doing in our rehearsals?"

"Fine," Wendy replied.

Felicia smiled. "Great. I thought I was doing all right, but I had to hear it from you."

"Why me?" Wendy asked.

"Because you're really good," Felicia replied. "I respect you, Wendy."

Wendy frowned as Felicia began to eat her lunch. She wasn't sure she could trust Felicia around Todd.

Felicia looked up at her. "What?"

"Nothing," Wendy replied. "I was just wondering how long you've known Todd."

"Not long," Felicia replied. "Listen, Wendy.

I've been hearing things all over school, about the drummers who used to play for your band."

"Like what?"

"Like, wow, you fired that Larry guy. And Paul, well, he had a couple of accidents."

"Does that bother you?" Wendy asked.

"I'm sorry about Paul," Felicia replied, "but I'm cool on everything else. I mean, this group is the most popular band in Cresswell. I'm lucky to be in it. I just hope nothing else happens to us."

Wendy smiled thinly. "Don't worry, Felicia. At this next gig, we won't have any platforms. Everything is going to be fine. I guarantee it."

With the Halloween dance rapidly approaching, Cathy stayed late every night after rehearsal. Jack tried to hang out with her, but Cathy always ran him off so she could work on her sound board. The time alone gave her a chance to think, to anticipate anything that might go wrong at the gig. She was going to make sure that nothing else happened to her band.

Cathy was pleased with their progress. Felicia had worked out well. The rest of them were cheerful, ready to strut their stuff again for the home team. Cathy knew they were the talk of the school—she had overheard more than one conversation in the hallways.

The garage was damp and cold with the October air. Wind rattled the dark windows. Cathy decided to go back into the house to get an electric space heater from her room.

As she walked across the yard, she heard a doorway creaking in the alley. Turning toward the noise, she peered into the shadows behind Margo's house. Her heart skipped a beat when Larry stepped into the alley.

He closed the door and started straight for her. Cathy hoped that he wouldn't see her, but as he turned the corner, he caught a glimpse of her standing there. Larry stopped and stared in her direction.

"What's the matter?" Cathy asked. "Ashamed to have anyone see you coming out of Margo's front door?"

Larry put his hands on his hips. "How's Heart of Stone?"

"The group is called Heart of Steel," Cathy replied.

"I was talking about *you!*"

Cathy flinched, but came back with another zinger. "We're playing the Halloween dance at school. They're paying us four hundred dollars. What are you doing these days?"

Larry folded his arms over his chest. "Margo and I are partying big time. She's a lot of fun. Not like my last girlfriend."

"Why don't you bring her to the dance?" Cathy said. "She can dress up as a two-timing little tramp. She won't even need a costume."

"Oh, I'm bringing her," Larry replied. "We can't wait to see you fall flat on your faces."

Cathy started to tremble. "Larry, you better not try anything at this gig. I mean it."

Larry just laughed and turned away, walking toward the street. After a moment, Cathy heard his motorcycle roaring off into the cold night, and she hurried into the house.

Up in her room, she thought about calling Jack or Wendy, but finally decided not to bother them. There was no need to upset everyone when things were going so well. She just wished there was some way to get rid of the bad feeling that Larry's hostile laughter had left behind.

Halloween fell on the Saturday of an important football game against Marshfield. Cresswell won big, taking over the lead in the local conference. The victory made the Halloween dance even more kinetic. As soon as the doors opened at eight o'clock, the Cresswell High gym began to fill quickly.

Cathy stood in the wings, peering out at the crowd, looking for Larry and Margo. Larry's threatening laugh still rang in her ears. Was he going to try something?

"Look at them!"

Cathy jumped, startled. Jack had come up beside her. She shook her head. *I'm really on edge.*

"What's wrong?" Jack asked.

"You scared me."

"Sorry. Wow, look at them, Cat. They really want to see us. All dressed up for trick or treat."

"Yes, I just hope we get the treat."

"What?"

"Nothing," Cathy replied. "You better get ready."

Jack smiled and touched her hand. "How about a little kiss for luck?"

She frowned at him. "Jack . . ."

"Okay, okay. I'm sorry."

When he went back to the dressing room, Cathy looked out at the audience, studying the costumes and masks. Her eyes grew wide when she saw two ghosts making their way through the crowd. Larry's long black hair stuck out from under the ghost mask. The short girl walking beside him had to be Margo.

Cathy had to warn the group. As she hurried backstage, the cry went up from the anxious crowd.

"We want Steel! We want Steel!"

The members of the band gathered around Cathy. "Listen up," she told them. "Larry and Margo are here. They might try to cause trouble. Everyone be sure to be super-careful."

But they didn't seem to hear her.

Wendy's eyes were glowing. "Listen! They can't get enough of us."

"We're in demand!" Todd cried.

Darren grinned from ear to ear. "I'll be able to get a date after the dance. This is great."

Felicia lifted her drumsticks in the air. "I never knew it would be like this. Let's knock 'em dead."

Jack pointed toward the stage. "Places, guys. Rock it inside out!"

Cathy just shook her head and went to her

sound board. When the curtain rose, she hit the switch that bathed the stage in multicolored lights. Another switch sent red smoke billowing into the air. Cathy had designed the eerie effects herself.

The kids screamed for more. And they would get it in the second set. More than anyone had expected.

At the end of the first set, the group rushed off stage. Jack grabbed Cathy and gave her a big kiss. He was on fire with excitement.

"We're smoking!" Wendy cried.

Todd slapped hands with Darren. "We've never sounded better, my man."

Darren raised his fists in the air. "You guys are great! Listen to them. They love us."

Cathy laughed and put her arm around Darren's shoulder. She felt better now that they had gotten through one set. She hadn't even minded Jack's kiss. They were having fun again.

Felicia grabbed Todd and hugged him. "Thanks for getting me into this group, Todd!"

Wendy slid between them. "I love it. We're going to slay them at the Pavilion."

Cathy had her eye on the clock. "Get something to drink, guys. We're back on in ten minutes."

"If they let us wait that long," Wendy replied, laughing.

When the break was over, Cathy sent them

onto the stage. Jack, Todd, and Wendy picked up their guitars. Darren slid behind the keyboard.

"Hurry, Felicia," Cathy called.

Felicia walked carefully in the dim light. Her drum set was toward the front of the stage. As she got closer, she saw that one of her cymbals was out of place—the high hat had been moved.

"Darn it," she muttered.

Wendy looked back, frowning. "Felicia. Hurry!"

"Okay, okay."

Felicia had to reset the high hat fast before the curtain went up. She sat down on her stool, reaching for the cymbal. When her hand closed around the metal stand, an electric shock surged through her thin body.

The current bit deeply into Felicia. Her hair stood straight out. She shook with two hundred and twenty volts of electric death.

The other members of the group stood frozen into place with horror, but the curtain was rising anyway. Cathy switched on the multicolored lights, and the stomach-churning spectacle was revealed. "Oh, my God!" Cathy cried. Wild cheers rose from the audience.

"What an act!" someone in the crowd yelled. "Halloween!"

Suddenly the overloaded fuse box blew, sending the gym into darkness. People starting screaming and pushing against the stage in panic.

With the power cut off, Felicia fell to the floor. The skin on her hands had been charred to a deep black hue. The stinking smell of sizzling flesh hung in the air. Her blue tongue was sticking out of her mouth, and her eyes had bulged to the point of bursting.

Cathy rushed to Felicia's side, pushing through the gagging stench of cooked flesh. "Help! Somebody help her!"

One of the teacher-chaperones rushed onto the stage. He knew CPR, but it was too late. Felicia was quite, quite dead.

Chapter 8

A cold November wind blew over the cemetery, chilling Cathy's shoulders. Felicia's coffin was lowered into the ground.

Cathy couldn't believe that Felicia's death had been bad luck. Someone had killed her deliberately, but the sheriff hadn't been able to find any evidence. Hagen had questioned everyone again after the Halloween gig. Although someone had reported seeing a costumed figure backstage just before Felicia was electrocuted, the information was too vague to make an arrest. Officially, Felicia's death was due to a frayed electrical cord that had fallen against the cymbal stand.

In her own testimony, Cathy had sworn that she had not used any faulty electrical equipment, and the other band members had backed her up. The sheriff had written it off as a lack of caution— the band had simply been careless. No charges were being brought against anyone.

When Felicia was laid to rest, Cathy and the others turned away from the grave, piled into Todd's van, and left the cemetery. They were silent as they headed back to Cresswell.

Jack sat next to Cathy with his arm around her. Darren was sitting on the other side of the van. Todd and Wendy were in the front.

"You okay?" Jack asked Cathy.

She nodded, and closed her eyes. She kept seeing Larry's hair sticking out from under the ghost mask. Margo had been right beside him. Could they—or anyone else—have sneaked backstage without being detected? The stage had been dark when the lights were off. Was Larry the one who put the live wire against the cymbal stand?

"Cathy?"

She opened her eyes. They had already arrived at her house. Cathy sighed and climbed out of the van. She walked toward her house without looking back. There was nothing to say. Not for a while, anyway.

The phone was ringing when Cathy walked into the house, and she heard her mother answer it in the living room. "Cathy?"

"Coming, Mom. Hello?" she said blankly.

"Miss Malone, this is Vern Kreeger from WCRS radio. I was wondering if we can still count on Heart of Steel for the Battle of the Bands at the Pavilion. It's only a couple of weeks away, you know."

Cathy felt a sense of outrage. "How can you call me like this? We just buried our drummer!"

"Er, yes, I'm terribly sorry about that. Allow me to extend my condolences. I know you're upset, but the fact is, since your group has been in

. . . well, in the news, ticket requests have doubled. They want to see you, Cathy. I—"

Cathy slammed down the receiver. Tears flowed onto her cheeks. She was trapped in a nightmare.

"Are you all right?" her mother asked.

Cathy hugged her mother, sobbing on her shoulder. Her mother stroked her hair.

"You should rest, Cathy."

Mrs. Malone led her upstairs and Cathy fell onto her bed. She stared up at the ceiling, wondering why Larry had turned into a murderer. She wasn't sure that he had hurt Paul. And Jack could have taken the bolts from the platform at the junior-high gig. But she had clearly seen Larry and Margo at the Halloween dance, making them prime suspects in Felicia's death.

Were they really in on it together? Larry knew enough about electrical equipment to have rigged Felicia's death trap. But Cathy wasn't sure that Larry could really have killed Felicia. She wasn't sure about anything.

Cathy curled up on the bed, sobbing until she drifted off into a fitful sleep.

A little later that afternoon, Margo ran for the telephone. "Hello?"

"Hi, babe, it's me. Uh, something has come up. I can't make it over today. Maybe I'll see you in school tomorrow."

Margo sighed disappointedly. "Larry, I really need to see you."

"Well, I can't. I've got some other things to do. It's business."

"What kind of business?" she asked suspiciously.

"Music stuff."

She brightened a little. "Really? Are you going to get into another group? I mean, I could sing backup."

"Something like that. I have to go, babe. I'll call you tonight."

"Larry—"

But he had already hung up.

Margo fumed as she slammed down the phone. Her heart began to pound. Was he lying to her? What if Larry was going to see another girl?

"Cathy!"

Margo peered out the window, looking at Cathy's house. Cathy was the only one who could ruin all her plans, all her work. If Larry went back to Cathy, Margo would be back out in the cold. The real obstacle in her path was Cathy Malone!

Cathy saw Felicia and Paul coming toward her in the darkness. Their arms were outstretched, as if they were going to grab her. Ghoulish white faces leered at Cathy with their horrible death grins.

"You killed us," Paul screeched.

"It's all your fault, Cathy," Felicia moaned.

"No!" Cathy cried. "No!"

Cathy sat up in her bed, escaping from the nightmare. Sweat poured off her face. The dream had seemed so incredibly real. What was happening to her? She looked out her window. It was only late afternoon.

Cathy needed to talk to someone. Who could she call? Jack? No—she'd never be able to get rid of him then. The only one she felt at all close to was Wendy.

After climbing off the bed, she went into the hallway and dialed Wendy's number. Wendy's father answered and told Cathy to try Todd's house. Todd's mother told Cathy that Todd and Wendy had gone out to the store, but they would return shortly.

"Thank you, Mrs. Steele. Listen, do you mind if I come over? Cathy, Cathy Malone. Yes, tell Todd and Wendy to wait for me. I'm on my way."

Cathy hung up and went to the window. Long shadows were stretching over the streets of the Upper Basin. She would have to walk to Todd's house in the rapidly falling dusk. Returning to her room, she grabbed her coat and ran downstairs.

"Where are you going?" her mother called.

"For a walk," Cathy replied.

She emerged from the house into the cool autumn air. She turned left, following the sidewalk toward Gaspee Farms. When she got to Todd's house, she could talk to him and Wendy about her suspicions. Maybe they could work together to catch Larry—or at least stop him from killing anyone else.

Gaspee Farms was the next neighborhood over from the Upper Basin. Cathy was cold, and her feet had begun to hurt as she passed Gaspee Place, a small shopping center. She had never been to Todd's house before, but she knew the address. Turning the corner, she headed for a large white house at the end of a cul-de-sac.

Todd's van was parked in the driveway of the house. Cathy was about to cross the street when she saw someone moving in the shadows ahead of her. She stopped dead on the sidewalk and caught her breath, then ducked quickly behind a tree.

The person in the shadows seemed to be watching Todd's place. Cathy squinted in the darkness until the figure shifted under the dim reflection of a streetlight.

"No!" Cathy said softly.

She recognized the long hair and the lanky build. Larry Hart was stalking another member of the band. Cathy had arrived just in time. Todd was his next victim!

Larry Hart gazed through the shadows, studying Todd Steele's brightly lit house. Larry wasn't really sure why he had come here. He only knew he was tired of seeing his former group getting hammered. Larry had hated them for a while, until trouble came down on them. Now he was anxious to find out who was so determined to destroy them.

Larry figured they all probably thought *he* was causing the trouble. But he knew he hadn't killed anyone. He felt sorry for Felicia and Paul, and he wanted to get even with whoever had killed them.

But who had done it? Everybody in the group was a suspect, even Cathy. After all, she had trashed the drums before he played. She might've pulled the platform job herself.

Shivering in the cool air, he watched the glowing windows of Todd's house. Larry wouldn't be able to get inside as long as everyone was home. There was only one thing to do—search Todd's van.

"Just get it over with," he muttered to himself.

Starting forward, he took one step into the street. Just then someone rushed up from behind him. Larry turned as the assailant leapt onto his back.

"What the—"

The killer had come to get *him!* His attacker hung on, slapping his head and shoulders. Larry spun around, trying to throw off the intruder. Suddenly, a female voice burned in his ear.

"You jerk! Stay away from Todd! Stay away from my band!"

"Cathy! Stop it!"

She wouldn't let go of him. Larry whirled around and around, trying to shake her loose. He saw a black shape out of the corner of his eye. Turning quickly, he slammed Cathy into a wide oak tree. She grunted and let go.

Larry wheeled to face her. Cathy leaned against the tree trunk, gasping to regain her breath. Larry grabbed her shoulders and pinned her to the tree.

"What do you think you're doing?" he rasped.

Cathy squirmed to free herself. "Let go of me! Ouch—"

He put his hand over her mouth and Cathy's eyes grew wide. He was going to hurt her. Her body trembled with fear. But Larry didn't want to hurt anyone, least of all the girl he regretted leaving.

He leaned closer to her, whispering, "I'll take my hand off your mouth if you promise not to scream."

Cathy nodded. Larry removed his hand, but he still kept her pinned to the oak tree.

"Damn you, Larry! Let me go, you big ape!"

"Not till I get some answers," Larry replied. "What did you think you were doing, anyway?"

"I—I saw you heading for Todd's van. I—I know you're the one, Larry. You were there at both gigs. I saw you. I'm going to turn you in!"

Larry sighed. "Cathy, I haven't killed anyone, I swear. I couldn't kill anyone if I wanted to."

"Then why were you stalking Todd? Why are you sneaking around here at night?"

"Hey, *you* attacked *me!*"

"Don't change the subject. I want the truth, Larry."

"I don't know, Cathy. I wasn't going to hurt Todd. I swear. I just want to find out who killed Paul and Felicia."

"What?"

He looked into her blue eyes. "I've been a real jerk, Cathy, but I didn't kill anyone."

"Prove it," Cathy challenged. "Let go of me."

He relaxed his grip, backing away from her. "There. You're free to go."

Cathy felt an urge to run. But she stayed, looking at him. She wasn't sure what to think. Larry turned away from her, looking back at Todd's place.

Cathy stiffened. "So you're saying you didn't cause any of the trouble at those two gigs?"

He laughed and shook his head. "Oh, I caused trouble. Big time. But I didn't make that platform collapse. And I didn't hurt Felicia."

"I saw you at the Halloween dance," Cathy accused. "You were in a costume, but I recognized you. Margo was with you."

He nodded. "I was there. But I left right before the end of the first set. I wasn't around when Felicia—well, when it happened."

"Right," Cathy replied. "You probably split after you rigged that electric death trap."

He spun back toward her. "No way."

"I can't believe you, Larry."

"That's *your* problem," he replied. "Besides, you were the one who trashed that drum set at the junior-high gig. How do I know you didn't rig the platform? I could've been in the cast instead of Paul. Tell me that."

"I didn't," Cathy insisted. "I would never hurt anyone in my own band. How can you think I did?"

"I don't," Larry replied. "Not really. But I didn't do anything, either."

She wasn't ready to give up. "I saw you at the hospital! You could have come back the next day and pushed Paul off the roof!"

"No way! I was in Porterville that night. I went down to hear another group with Steve and Billy. Just ask them!"

They were quiet for a moment. A cool breeze wrapped around them.

As Larry exhaled, his breath fogged the night air. "Cathy, I—I'm sorry. I didn't kill anyone. But I know someone was responsible for what happened to Paul and Felicia. And I can't just sit back and let them get away with it."

Cathy hesitated. She was almost starting to believe him. She wanted to think he was telling the truth. He seemed so sincere. It was a whole new side of him—a caring side. But what if Larry was just trying to cover for himself?

"All right," she said finally. "If you really want to help, then go to the sheriff and tell him everything you know."

"I did! After the junior-high gig, I told Hagen what I had done. I was honest with him. I said that I came with my friends to make you let me play."

"What about the Halloween dance?" Cathy challenged. "You were there."

"I told you, I left before the first set was over."

"Why did you come in the first place?"

"I wanted to see the band," he replied. "And I

thought somebody might try something. But when nothing happened, I felt stupid and I left. I wasn't the one who set that frayed cable."

Cathy's eyes grew narrow. "How did you know it was a frayed cable?"

"Cathy! It was all over the paper and the television. Somebody *had* to rig it like that."

"Yeah? Why?"

He smiled a little. "Because I know that you would never use defective equipment. That's not your style. You're too cautious. You double-check everything. You'd never be that careless."

She lowered her eyes. "You really do know me," she said softly.

He grabbed her arms. "Cathy, you're right in a way. This is all my fault. I—I blew it, with the group and with you. I—"

"Larry, don't . . ."

"No, Cat, I mean it. I lost you. I was stupid to go after Margo. I—I'm sorry. That's all I can say."

Cathy sighed deeply. "Wow. I'd like to believe you, Larry. I—"

He shook his head. "I wouldn't blame you if you didn't. I want to make it right, Cat. But I can't do it by myself. I need your help. I—I need you. I want you back, Cat."

Cathy drew back. "One thing at a time, Larry. I'd like to think you really want to help. But tell me what's on your mind about the murders."

"Okay," Larry replied. "This is how it goes. . . ."

* * *

Margo waited at the window a long time before she saw Cathy coming down the sidewalk. She couldn't see Cathy's face under the street lamp, but she knew it was her. Cathy turned onto her front walk and hurried into the house next to Margo's.

She had been with Larry! Margo knew it. They were seeing each other again.

Margo picked up the telephone and dialed. Larry answered.

"It's me," Margo said. "Where have you been?"

"Like I told you," he replied, "doing business."

"With Cathy?"

When he hesitated at the other end of the line, Margo knew that he had been with the other girl.

"You rat!" she cried.

"Look, Margo, it's none of your business who I was with. Okay? No hard feelings, but I don't think we should see each other for a while."

Margo quickly got a rein on her temper. She knew what she had to do if she was going to hang on to Larry.

"Margo?"

"Larry, please, I'm sorry. Don't be mad at me."

"I'm not mad, Margo. It's just—something has come up. I won't be able to see you right now."

"Larry," she said in a soft tone, "come over. I can make you feel better. I can give you what you want."

"Margo, there's more to life than getting what

112

you want. I'm sorry. Look, I'll see you around. We can still be friends, okay?"

Margo slammed down the phone. "Friends? No way, José. I'll never call you or Cathy my friend."

Cathy was the problem. If not for her, Margo would have kept Larry, and she would have gotten into the band. Cathy was hurting her. Cathy had to pay.

Cathy closed the door to her room. She lay back on the bed, staring up at the ceiling. Everything was so mixed up. She wanted to believe Larry, and she still had feelings for him, but she couldn't trust him.

After listening to his plan in the darkness, Cathy was almost convinced that it would work. It would take some doing, and it wouldn't be easy.

But she knew she had to put her emotions on hold if their plan was going to work. She sat up on the bed, already committed to the idea. It was going to take a great deal of maneuvering. She wasn't sure she could convince everyone else to go along with the plan.

Cathy heard the phone ringing, and her mother called to her from downstairs. Cathy went into the hall, picking up the extension.

"Cathy? Hi, this is Vern Kreeger again. Listen, I wanted to apologize to you for this afternoon. I didn't mean to—"

"No," Cathy replied. "It's all right. I was going to call you back."

"Then you are interested in playing at the Battle of the Bands?"

"We're interested, Mr. Kreeger. But you'll have to give me some time. Is that all right?"

"Sure, Cathy. Whatever you say. Call me Vern. Listen, when will you know for sure?"

"Give me a few days. I'll let you know soon."

"Great, Cathy. I'm looking forward to it."

She hung up, taking a deep breath. It was going to be tricky, but the wheels were in motion. Now all she had to do was present the package to Heart of Steel.

Chapter 9

Cathy raised the stainless-steel ax and brought it down hard on the piece of wood, splitting it in half. Her mother had had the fireplace and the chimney cleaned, so they needed firewood. Cathy was glad to get the exercise, because it took her mind off the meeting later that afternoon.

She split another stick of cord wood. The ax was sharp and the steel handle made it strong, almost impossible to break. A sweat broke on her forehead as she finished piling up the armload of wood.

"This should be enough," she muttered to herself.

Walking back to the garage, she put the ax on the wall, resting it between two nails next to the door. Then she gathered up the pile of wood. Her mother was in the kitchen when Cathy walked in with her arms full.

"Good Lord, Cathy, you've been hard at work."

"Yes, ma'am. We can have a fire tonight."

She started for the living room.

"Cathy?"

She turned back toward her mother. "Yes, Mom?"

"Cathy, are you having another meeting with that band today?"

Cathy nodded. "At two o'clock."

Her mother sighed. "Cathy, there's been an awful lot of trouble. Maybe you shouldn't—I mean, I'm not forbidding you to do it, mind you, but it might be a good idea to leave it alone for a while."

"It's okay, Mom. We're just going to talk. Everything is going to be all right."

"Just be careful, dear."

"I will."

Cathy went into the living room and stored the wood next to the fireplace. She stacked some logs in the hearth and lit them with a long match. The kindling sparked to life, raising high flames that licked the flue opening. Cathy sat there for a while, transfixed by the hypnotic flickering of the fire.

Heart of Steel was gathered again in Cathy's garage.

Jack did his best to stay next to Cathy. He was surprisingly upbeat after all that had happened. Cathy did her best to stay away from him. She didn't want to offer any more encouragement.

Todd and Wendy sat together on a pair of milk crates. They were laughing and talking about a concert they had seen the night before. The band hadn't been nearly as good as Steel, no competition at all.

Darren leaned back against the door with a half-smile on his face. He had been dating one of the groupies who followed the band. Now that the group enjoyed some notoriety, Darren was one of the most popular kids at Cresswell.

Cathy was surprised that they were all so unaffected by Felicia's death. It had been only a week since the funeral, but they were acting as if nothing had happened. Cathy decided to shake them up.

She clapped her hands together. "Okay, guys. You may not like this, but there's someone I want you to meet."

Jack squinted at her. "Who?"

Cathy moved to the garage door. She opened it and waved out into the yard. After a moment, Larry stepped into the garage. A collective groan rose in the air.

Jack bristled, and glared at Cathy. "You've got to be kidding."

Todd jumped to his feet. "I'm out of here. Come on, Wendy. Let's split."

"No," Wendy replied. "Let's wait a minute. Cathy—"

"Please," Cathy went on. "I want you to listen to Larry. I think he has some ideas about what happened to Paul and Felicia."

Jack hated the fact that his competition had returned. "What's he going to tell us? That he killed our drummers?"

Larry tried to stay calm. "No, I didn't kill anyone, Jack. But someone did. And if you walk out on me now, you're just as bad as the killer."

Jack took a threatening step toward Larry. "I don't have to take this."

Cathy stepped between them. "No, Jack! Listen to him. If you really care about me and this group, you'll stay."

Jack hesitated, then backed away. "All right, Cathy. If that's what you want."

"I'm sorry, Jack," Larry went on. "Don't go. You've got to listen to me."

Jack looked at Cathy with hurt on his face. "Do you really trust this guy, Cathy?"

She nodded. "Yes, I think so."

I bet you still love him, too! Jack thought.

"We need each other," Larry said. "Somebody killed Paul and Felicia. What if one of us is next?"

"Yeah, right," Jack snapped. "What if *you're* the one who's going to do it?"

Larry sighed deeply. "You're wrong, Jack. I know I caused trouble at the junior-high gig, but I didn't trash that platform. And I wasn't even in Cresswell when Paul went off that roof."

"What about Felicia?" Jack challenged. "You could have set the cord that electrocuted her."

"I admit that I was at the dance that night, but I left before Felicia was killed."

"So what are you doing here now?" Darren asked.

"I have a plan to trap the killer," Larry replied. "But I need all of you to help me."

"Us?" Jack said.

"We have to keep the band together," Larry replied. "We have to play again. It's the only way to draw out the killer."

Jack shook his head and glanced at Cathy. "He's finally bugged out, Cathy. He's lost it."

Wendy glared at Jack. "Oh, shut up, Akers. Listen to Larry. I think he's onto something."

"Thanks," Larry replied. "Now, think about it. Someone wanted to hurt the band, and they were successful. But if the group breaks up, the killer will be off the hook. I mean, if I *had* done it, would I want to bring us together? If Steel was finished, the killer would walk free. I wouldn't draw attention to myself by trying to get back in the band. I may be a little crazy, but I'm not completely stupid."

Wendy nodded. "Larry has a point. It does make sense to keep the band together."

Jack grunted and scowled at Wendy. "Yeah? Well, what if he's trying to keep the band together so he can kill us all? We could never trust him."

"I'm here now," Larry replied. "I've got nothing to hide. How about you, Akers? Have you got something to hide?"

Jack turned to Cathy. "He's nuts. Come on, Cathy, let's get out of here. We don't have to take this."

Cathy shook her head. "Jack—I'm with Larry on this. And what about the rest of you? Huh? Someone in this room could be the killer."

Larry looked straight at Jack. "And the killer would want to keep the band from getting back together."

Suddenly, they were all staring at Jack.

"No way!" Jack cried.

Wendy stood up. "Larry's right, Jack. You seem to be hung up on the band not playing again. Have you got something to hide?"

"No!" Jack replied.

"Please," Cathy said. "Do it for me, Jack."

Jack took a deep breath. "Okay, say we do get back together. We don't even have another gig."

Cathy nodded. "Yes, we do. Bridgewater. The Battle of the Bands still wants us. We can play the Pavilion in a couple of weeks, but I have to tell the promoter today. We have to make it official."

A smile spread over Wendy's face. "The Pavilion. That would be great. How can we turn it down? And Larry is the only drummer who could play with us on such short notice."

"Probably the only drummer who would want to play," Todd said.

"I still don't trust him," Jack growled.

Larry glared back at him. "You don't have much choice."

"Bite it, Hart!"

"Look," Larry replied, "I'm going to keep searching for the killer no matter what you do, Jack. The best way to do that is to keep playing. We can all watch out for each other. And if the killer tries again—"

"We'll catch him!" Wendy said.

They were quiet for a moment. Jack was fuming. Todd and Darren were thoughtful, and Wendy seemed to be behind Larry all the way.

They all looked at each other, doubts swirling in their heads. Larry was right about one thing, Cathy thought—they needed each other if they were going to survive.

"Let's vote on it," Cathy said finally.

Wendy raised her hand immediately. "I say we stay together and play the Pavilion gig. Come on, guys, get with it."

Cathy lifted her hand. "I'm in."

"Me, too," Darren said.

Todd raised his hand. "I'm with Wendy. I think Larry is right. We've got to play this gig."

Jack snorted and reluctantly gave in. "All right, Hart. But I'm going to be watching you. You better not get out of line."

"The same goes for you, Akers," Larry replied.

"Then it's unanimous," Cathy said.

Heart of Steel would play again.

Margo stood in the shadows, watching as four of the group members left the garage. She felt hot and angry in the cool night. Larry was still inside the garage with Cathy.

Margo slipped up next to the half-opened door. She could hear their voices, and the dialogue made her sick.

"Cathy," Larry said, "I'm glad it finally worked out."

"Don't be so sure," Cathy replied. "We still have to play the Pavilion."

Larry was back in the group. He had betrayed her after all she had done for him! Margo hated him.

"What about us, Cathy?"

"Larry, I'm not sure there is an 'us.' I mean . . ."

"It's okay. If nothing else, Cat, I want us to be friends. I want you to respect me again, if that's possible."

Margo had heard enough. She hurried through the shadows to the back door of her house.

"You two-timing jerk," she said under her breath. "No more! I'll show them."

The next day at school, Wendy was sitting in the cafeteria when three younger girls approached her. They were giggling and blushing as if they were embarrassed. Wendy smiled at them and said hello.

"Are you Wendy Coles?" one of them asked.

"Yes, I am."

"See, I told you."

"Wow, she's a real rock star."

"You're in Heart of Steel."

Wendy nodded, her eyes aglow with stardom.

"We were wondering—could you get us some tickets for the Battle of the Bands at the Pavilion?"

"Yeah, we're big fans of yours. Would you sign my notebook?"

Wendy frowned, feigning disappointment. "I'm sorry, kids, I can't really get any tickets. But I'll be happy to give you my autograph."

"Wow, that would be great."

Wendy signed her name for them and they ran off, giggling. Wendy felt great. She was finally starting to get some of the recognition she deserved. She was really looking forward to the Pavilion gig.

The Battle of the Bands was an all-day affair. Ten rock-and-roll groups played before a panel of five judges who were disc jockeys from local radio stations. The competition came in two stages. Beginning at noon, the ten bands each played a half-hour set. The first round usually lasted until six-thirty or seven o'clock in the evening.

After the first round, the judges would take a break and choose three bands for the second show that night. The finalists would each play a forty-five-minute set, and the winner would be chosen to receive the first prize of five thousand dollars.

Even if a band didn't win, there was still plenty of local exposure, and some record people would be coming from New York. Win or lose, the Battle of the Bands had the unreal air of a big-time gig. Wendy could hear the applause and cheers as she rose to the top of the rock scene.

Another voice drifted across the cafeteria to disturb her daydreaming. "Look, that's Wendy Coles."

"What a fox."

"Man, I hope I can get tickets for the Battle."

"Yeah, I can't wait to see what happens. It's like Steel has risen from the grave."

Wendy smiled. "We're on our way," she whispered to herself. "And nothing can stop us. Nothing."

Darren Quick gazed at himself in the mirror. The day of the Pavilion gig had arrived, and he wanted to look good. His new girlfriend was going to be in the audience.

He smiled at himself. "Looking good, Quick."

His hair was longer, and he had bought new wire-rimmed glasses. Nerd-boy was gone forever. No one laughed at him now.

Darren wasn't really thinking about any danger that might threaten the band. He had decided that Felicia and Paul had died in unfortunate accidents. The band's luck was due to change—their rehearsals had been going well for nearly two weeks. They couldn't lose.

"Five thousand dollars," he said to himself.

His share would come to over eight hundred dollars. Darren could buy a car. He would never have to ride the school bus again.

"Eight big ones," he said to the mirror.

He could already feel the money in his pocket.

Jack Akers paced back and forth in his room. He was anxious, but not about the Pavilion gig. The band sounded great. It was Cathy who made him nervous.

"Freaking Larry Hart!"

Jack hated Larry more than anyone he had ever known. He had been sure that Cathy and he would get together, but then Larry came back into the group. Now Jack's chances were dwindling to nothing. Cathy didn't even seem to need his protection anymore.

Larry was playing the game perfectly. He wasn't being cocky. He was the model of cooperation, keeping his mouth shut, showing up on time for all their rehearsals.

Cathy was warming up to Larry again. Jack felt a pain in his chest every time Cathy and Larry exchanged smiles. Cathy should be smiling at *him!*

"That geek!"

Jack wanted to fix Larry, but good. He could take Larry's head off. But in his imagination, he saw Cathy kneeling next to Larry's bloody body, offering him her sympathies.

There was nothing for Jack to do but go through with the gig. The five-thousand-dollar first prize didn't even enter his thoughts. He could only fume about the girl who didn't love him and the guy who had taken her away.

"Man, this stinks."

Spinning around quickly, he threw his fist into the wall. The plaster cracked under the force of the blow. Jack drew back his fist. It was covered with blood and flakes of plaster.

"That should be your face, Hart."

Larry had ruined it for Jack. How could Cathy

125

go for that greasy biker? And to make things worse, the band sounded better with Larry on the drums!

Jack hurried out of his room, heading for the bathroom so he could wash the blood from his hand.

Todd pulled up in front of Wendy's house in Rocky Bank Estates. When he honked the horn, Wendy came out, running toward the van. Todd's eyes grew wide. She was dressed in a black leather outfit that he had never seen before.

"Wendy, you look— Wow!"

She smiled. "Thanks. We better hurry."

Todd put the van in gear and drove away from her house. "Wendy, where did you get that suit?"

"You like it?"

"I don't know." She almost looked *too* hot.

Wendy laughed. "Don't worry, Todd. I just want to look good. This isn't for anyone's benefit."

Wendy stared out the window, thinking of how she would spend the prize money. Her family would be so proud of her when she brought home the eight hundred dollars. And that would only be the start!

"Todd," she said wistfully, "have you ever ridden in a limousine?"

"No."

"Well, you will someday. After we're famous. It'll be great, the crowds cheering, the fans wanting our autographs."

Todd smiled a little, letting himself run with the fantasy. "Yeah, touring, videos—MTV!"

"We'll be on the cover of *People* magazine!"

"Nah," Todd replied. *"Rolling Stone.* Or *Spin!"*

"Speed it up, Todd," Wendy told him. "We don't want to be late."

Todd pressed down on the accelerator. They had to pick up the others and get to Bridgewater. It was going to be the best day of his life.

Wendy leaned back, gazing out the window, never considering the possibility that something might happen to ruin all of her dreams.

All morning, Cathy had been in her garage going over the song list for the Pavilion gig. She felt good about the band's sound. They had really been cooking in rehearsals. Larry had been a perfect angel, and the others had accepted him—except for Jack, who rarely said a word to him.

Cathy still had her doubts about Jack. She wondered if he could have had something to do with the "accidents." Jack had a nasty temper that had been coming out more and more lately.

Cathy looked up suddenly from her sound board. She had heard a noise outside the garage, like someone was trying to sneak up on her. Moving quickly toward the door, she picked up the stainless-steel ax that hung on the wall. She held her breath as the door began to swing open.

"Cathy?" Larry called into the garage.

She returned the ax to the wall. "Larry. I didn't hear your motorcycle."

Larry pushed into the garage. "I walked over. I'm a little nervous. How about you?"

Cathy nodded. "Yeah, pins and needles."

Larry held out his arms. Cathy embraced him, putting her head on his chest. She felt torn. She wanted the band to sound good, but she was nervous that something would happen.

Fans and critics were whispering about Steel all over Cresswell, and they weren't talking about the group's talent. Well, maybe their talent at getting killed. Cathy wasn't even thinking about the five thousand dollars. She just wanted them to get out of the gig alive.

She drew back from Larry. "We have to be careful."

"I'll be right there," he replied. "I won't let you down."

Their eyes locked for a moment. Cathy wanted him to kiss her, but their lips didn't meet. Outside, Todd honked the horn of his van, calling them to the gig in Bridgewater.

Wendy's eyes were glittering with excitement as she scanned the rafters of the Bridgewater Pavilion. "It's so big. Huge!"

Todd smiled and put his hand on her shoulder. "It *is* awesome. Almost scary."

Darren's eyes were wide. "Wow. I think we've hit the big time."

"Right," Jack scoffed. "We only drove fifteen miles from Cresswell to get here. I wouldn't call that the big time." He turned to glare at Larry and Cathy, who stood together.

Cathy was awed by the fifty-foot ceilings of the Pavilion arena. The place seated almost ten thousand people at full capacity, and it was going to be packed for the Battle of the Bands. All the tickets had been sold out for a week.

Larry shook his head. "I didn't remember it being this humongous."

"Too humongous," Cathy replied, gazing toward the proscenium arch.

On the stage, technicians and stagehands were setting up for the concert. There had to be fifty people at work, creating an atmosphere of confusion.

Todd pointed toward the stage. "Look at all the equipment. Man, we could never afford that much stuff."

The guitarists and keyboard players had all brought their own instruments, but because of the ten groups and the time constraints, all the groups had to share the same amplifiers, microphones, and drums.

Cathy's hand had begun to tremble. "There're too many people here. If somebody is out to get us—"

"Lighten up," Wendy said. "It's going to be okay. Nobody will try anything."

"Maybe Cathy is right," Jack said, trying to sound sympathetic all of a sudden. "I think—"

Wendy glared at him. "I don't care what you think, Jack. We're going through with this gig. If you want to chicken out, then hit the road. Darren can play the bass notes on his organ."

"Get off me, Wendy," Jack said. "I can—"

"Hey, what are you kids doing here?"

The voice had come from the aisle between the rows of seats, interrupting Jack's angry words.

They all turned to look at a small, thin man who moved down the aisle toward them. He was dressed in blue jeans, a black T-shirt, and a black satin jacket with "Pavilion Staff" embroidered in red thread on the front. He carried a clipboard by his side.

"You kids clear out," the man told them. "Nobody's allowed in here for another two hours."

"We're not fans," Cathy said quickly. "We're Heart of Steel. We're here to play."

The man's hostile expression changed to a smarmy smile. "Yeah? I'm Vern Kreeger. You guys were supposed to come through the backstage door."

Cathy shrugged. "We weren't sure where to come in. But we're here now. I'm Cathy Malone."

Kreeger gave them the once-over, his eyes lingering on Wendy. "So, you're the Steel that everyone has been talking about. Somehow I expected you to be older. Oh, well, I've got good news, kids. Because you're so popular, we're going to put you on last. You're the big finale, the star act."

Wendy grinned at Kreeger. "The star act! Wow."

Kreeger winked at her. "Yeah, and you look the part, babe."

Jack wasn't ready to give up his bad mood. "Last? That stinks."

"Relax, big guy," Kreeger replied. "Going last gives you a better chance with the judges. By the time you get on, they'll have forgotten all about your competition. You've got the inside track."

"Yeah, Jack," Wendy rejoined. "Shut up already."

Kreeger kept his eyes on Wendy. "Listen, kids, I know you've had some bad luck, but we've got plenty of backstage security to look out for you. You're kind of notorious, but that sells tickets."

Wendy looked at the others. "Did you hear that? My man here says it's okay. We're going to be fine."

"I like your attitude, gorgeous," Kreeger replied. "Come on, I'll show you to your dressing room. You may want to take it easy. It's going to be a long day."

He moved off down the aisle, heading for the stage. Wendy took Todd's arm, and they followed after Kreeger. Darren fell in behind them, but Jack lingered, looking at Cathy.

"Let's go, Cathy," Jack said.

"Uh, I'll be right there," Cathy replied. "I want to talk to Larry for a moment."

A sneer spread over Jack's rugged face. "Yeah, right. The two lovebirds. Who needs it?" He stormed off down the aisle.

"Caveman city," Larry said.

Cathy took Larry's arm. "I'm worried about Jack," she whispered. "I think he might've trashed that platform at the j-high gig so you would fall, Larry."

"I was thinking the same thing," Larry replied. "I'll keep an eye on him."

As they started after the others, Cathy felt the butterflies in her stomach. The stage was full of strangers; a killer could get lost in the shuffle. Heart of Steel had to play on that stage. And they were going to be the final act, which meant that they had to wait all day for the ax to fall.

"Excuse me," the guard said at the backstage door, "may I see your pass?"

Margo Reardon turned her eyes on the guard, forcing a smile. "I'm with the band. It's okay."

The guard shook his head. "No pass, no entry."

"I'm with the band," Margo repeated impatiently. "Isn't my name on the list? Cathy Malone, I'm with Heart of Steel."

The guard looked at his clipboard. "Malone, Malone. Oh yeah, you're right here. Cathy Malone, Heart of Steel."

Margo started to move past him. "Thanks."

He put his hand on her shoulder. "Can I see some identification?"

Margo glared at him. "I left my purse inside. I was here earlier this morning, but I had to go out. Okay?"

He glanced down at the cloth sack that Margo held in her hand. "What's in the bag?"

Margo sighed impatiently. "Some cords, guitar strings, and electrical tape. I had to get them for my group. Here, take a look."

Margo opened the bag, giving him a hasty glance. The guard wasn't sure what he saw, but the fact that she showed him was convincing enough.

"Okay, sorry, Miss Malone. You can go through."

Margo hurried into the shadows of the back-stage area. Her heart was pounding as she pulled the bag close to her. The guard hadn't recognized the components for a firebomb.

Margo slipped through the crowd, finding a dark alcove where she could sit unnoticed. She wasn't sure she could do it. It would be hard with all the people around.

Then she saw Cathy and Larry walking through the wings, and she knew that Heart of Steel had to die.

Chapter 10

Jack Akers paced back and forth in the small cubicle of a dressing room. He kept glancing at the clock on the wall. It was only ten after one. Six more bands had to play before Heart of Steel got their chance.

The other members of the group were sitting in folding chairs. Darren sipped his soft drink. Todd had his arm around Wendy's shoulders. Larry sat next to Cathy, which really infuriated Jack. Cathy had her eyes closed, trying to fight back her nerves.

Jack suddenly stopped pacing and slammed his fist against the wall. "This really bites it. This dressing room is too hot. Something is going to happen, I can feel it."

Larry sprang to his feet. "I've had about enough of your mouth, Akers. If you don't like it, take a walk. We don't need you."

Jack lunged at Larry. They began to wrestle, bumping into the walls.

"Stop it, both of you!" Cathy cried. "This isn't going to help us."

"Cathy's right," Wendy said. "There are ten

thousand people out there waiting to hear us. If we don't . . ."

Wendy's voice trailed off, and she turned her head toward the dressing-room door. A dull roar rose from the Pavilion arena. The vibrations shook the whole building.

"What is it?" Cathy asked.

They weren't sure what they heard at first. But then the chant became clear, echoing through the Pavilion.

Wendy's face came alive with the sudden glow of elation. "My God, they're chanting for us."

The audience had begun to call for them. "We want Steel! We want Steel!"

It would be a while before the crowd finally got what they wanted.

Vern Kreeger stuck his head into the dressing room. "Okay, Steel, you're up."

They all turned toward the door. The wait had seemed like an eternity.

Larry grabbed Cathy's hand. "Let's do it!"

Jack glared at him. "You better not blow it, Hart."

Wendy felt like she was walking on a cloud. "Let's knock them dead, guys."

Todd gave her a quick kiss. "They're gonna love you, babe."

Darren pushed his glasses onto the bridge of his nose. "I feel weak."

"You'll be okay," Cathy replied. "Come on, let's go."

As they left the dressing room, the second-to-last act was coming off the stage. They glared at the members of Steel, the infamous band from Cresswell.

"Hostile dudes," Todd said.

Wendy laughed. "Can you blame them? I mean, who wants to play when the crowd is calling *our* name?"

In single file, they slipped down the dim aisle and onto the stage. Cathy held her breath as they plugged in their instruments, but they were fine. She turned away, hurrying toward the sound board on the left side of the stage. But when she got there, a tall blond guy was watching the meters as the group tuned their instruments.

"Uh, I think that's my job," Cathy said.

The guy shook his head. "Not today."

"Hey, listen . . ."

Vern Kreeger came up beside her. "Problem?"

"Yes," Cathy replied, "he won't let me mix my group."

"Sorry, Cathy," Kreeger replied. "Nobody handles the sound board but Jimmy. It's the only way to be fair to the groups who don't have sound people."

Cathy agreed with his reasoning, but she was still disappointed. Moving back toward the stage, she found a place where she could watch. Oh, well. Maybe it was better that she could keep an eye on them while they played, anyway.

The announcer's voice came over the public address system. "And now—Heart of Steel!"

As the curtain went up, the cheers of the audience were deafening. Todd came to life, sliding forward into a heavy-metal lead. When the rest of the band followed, the fans settled down, listening to the music.

Cathy wasn't completely satisfied with the mix, but it was better than nothing. The group slipped smoothly into the second number, with Cathy nervously twisting her hands together. But there were no mishaps, and the thirty-minute set flew by. The group finished with booming bass, screaming guitars, howling organ, and crashing drums.

The curtain dropped quickly, and the audience began to boo and throw things at the stage. They chanted for more, but there were no encores at the Battle of the Bands.

Heart of Steel came off stage, jumping up and down, congratulating each other. Even Jack seemed happier, although he didn't look at Larry when he threw his arms around Cathy and kissed her. They were ecstatic! They were a hit!

But the good mood wouldn't last forever.

Margo sat back in the shadows, crying. She hadn't found the courage to set off the firebomb. She had already made a decision about the second half of the competition—if Heart of Steel made the finals, Margo was going to torch the place.

The audience was cheering, waiting for the announcement. Margo hated them all. They should have been cheering for her!

The voice came over the public-address system. "And now, the three finalists. And they are —from Marshfield, The Cree-tones. From Union City, Marshmallow Intestines. And, from Cresswell, Heart of Steel!"

The audience cheered wildly and began to chant, "We want Steel!"

Margo dried her tears.

"You see," Wendy said to Cathy, "I told you everything was going to be all right."

Cathy nodded. She still couldn't escape the feeling that disaster was present in every movement, every vague shape that shifted in the backstage shadows. Things had gone *too* well for the bad-luck band.

"Where are the guys?" Cathy asked. "We're on in a few minutes."

"I'll get them," Wendy replied. "I hope Jack and Larry aren't fighting again."

As Cathy waited in the wings, she told herself that it would be nice to finish, get the heck out of Bridgewater, maybe even win the five thousand dollars. She could relax only after the gig was over.

The group came up behind her. They were energetic, jumping, ready to go. Cathy was proud of their professionalism. They had survived a lot to make it to the finals.

As soon as the group onstage had finished, the audience began their chant.

Then the announcer came on and grabbed a mike. "And now, Heart of Steel!"

The group rushed onto the stage as the curtain went up. Todd plugged in his guitar and stepped up to the microphone. His lonely guitar riff filled the air with a solemn melody. The rest of the band kicked in for a slow number, "Stark Reality," the tribute to Paul.

Todd's voice was haunting. "You've got to face —the stark ree-al-a-tee—"

When he finished the song, the audience didn't get a chance to applaud. The group went right into the next number, picking up the energy level. Wendy broke into a lively vocal.

Cathy's eyes shifted back and forth, focusing on the shadows behind the group. She froze for a moment when she saw the female shape crawling out from under the drummer's platform. Her heart began to pound when she recognized the girl.

"Margo!" It had been her all along!

Cathy started to move, but it was too late. A thunderous explosion resounded through the auditorium. Margo disappeared in a ball of flame. The stage shook as if it had been rocked with the force of an earthquake.

Smoke fumed in the air, filling the stage with a dense cloud. Instantly, there was panic in the arena. Screams rose everywhere, with people running around in dangerous confusion.

Cathy had been knocked down by the explosion, but she managed to get to her feet, staggering toward the stage to see if the band was still alive.

The explosion had thrown Larry off the drummer's platform. He was lying on his back at the center of the stage. The others were trying to lift him so they could carry him out of the burning auditorium.

Cathy rushed down the aisle between the flames and knelt over Larry. He opened his eyes weakly, but he was still alive.

Vern Kreeger ran up on stage behind them. "This way," he said. "Through the theater-scene shop."

Jack and Darren picked Larry up. They followed Kreeger through the smoke until they came to a narrow flight of steps that led downward.

"Where do these go?" Cathy asked.

"To the basement," Kreeger replied. "There's an exit down there."

"Are you sure?" Wendy cried.

Kreeger started down the steps. "You can stay if you want, but I'm saving my own butt."

"We have to go," Todd cried. "Stay together!"

With Larry in tow, the group moved carefully on the narrow concrete steps. There were no lights in the cellar, and it seemed to be getting hotter. Smoke swirled all around them.

"We're trapped!" Jack cried, then coughed as the smoke filled his lungs.

Cathy's eyes squinted through the smoke. "Kreeger!"

There was no reply from the darkness. They were going to die a horrible, fiery death.

"Kreeger!" Cathy screamed desperately.

A voice rolled through the smoke. "Over here!"

They began to move slowly toward the sound of the voice.

"The door is open!" Kreeger yelled.

They took a few more steps. Cathy tripped over something, falling to the floor. Wendy helped her to her feet.

"Hurry!"

When Cathy stood up, she saw a dim glow through the haze. A rush of cool air hit her face as the others moved ahead of her. Wendy led her through the open door into the night air.

Kreeger was waiting for them at the bottom of another set of concrete stairs. Wendy helped Cathy up the steps. They hurried to the edge of the parking lot where Jack, Todd, and Darren were hovering over Larry.

"Is he going to be all right?" Cathy asked.

"I don't know," Jack replied.

"He's breathing," Darren said.

Todd knelt next to Larry. "I think he's going to make it."

Wendy was gazing back at the clouds of smoke that billowed from the windows of the Pavilion. "The whole place is burning down."

"Wow," Darren said. "I wonder what happened."

"It was Margo," Cathy replied. "She did it."

She sat beside Larry, touching his darkened face. He was alive; that was all that mattered. She could already hear the sirens screeching through Bridgewater.

Sheriff Tommy Hagen, whose jurisdiction extended to Bridgewater, paced back and forth in front of Todd's van. The back door of the van was open. Cathy and Wendy sat on the floor of the vehicle with their legs dangling over the parking lot. Darren, Jack, and Todd flanked the girls, leaning on the van. Larry was already on his way to the hospital.

"More trouble," the sheriff said in a hostile voice. "And I find you kids in the middle of it all."

Cathy lifted her weary blue eyes. "Margo Reardon set that fire. I saw her climbing out from under the stage."

Hagen turned away, gazing at the building. "They were lucky the whole place didn't go up."

Fire trucks surrounded the building. The fire had been brought under control. A great deal of damage had been done to the stage area, but for the most part, the Pavilion had been saved.

The stampede by the audience had been more serious, injuring eighteen people. Miraculously, there had only been one death—a young woman who was discovered near the drummer's platform.

"We found the Reardon girl," Hagen said. "She's dead."

"I think she killed Felicia and Paul too, Sheriff," Cathy said dully. "Margo was at both of those gigs."

Wendy scowled and shook her head. "That stupid Margo. She ruined everything."

"It was Larry's fault," Jack said. "She was *his* girlfriend."

"No way," Cathy replied. "Larry was trying to help us, Sheriff. We let him back into the group so we could find out who was trying to kill us."

Hagen sighed wearily. "Well, it's over now. The Reardon girl is gone. But I'm afraid you kids can't play any more concerts in my county."

Todd frowned. "Man, that's bogus."

"Don't push me, kid," Hagen replied. "I'm letting you off scot-free. Thank God you got away with your life. In the meantime, shag your tails back to Cresswell and stay out of trouble."

Hagen walked away to join his deputies.

Darren shook his head. "Margo. Who would have thought it?"

"Come on," Cathy said. "I want to see Larry at the hospital."

"I'm not going to see *him,*" Jack said.

Wendy glared at him. "Oh, shut up, Jack. Can't you see Cathy is upset?"

"That's okay," Todd rejoined. "They took Larry back to Cresswell. We can drop Jack on the way."

"Suits me fine," Jack replied.

Cathy ignored Jack. She was desperate to find out how Larry was doing. Larry was the one she loved.

Chapter 11

Wendy, Todd, and Darren accompanied Cathy to Cresswell Community Hospital. The emergency room was busy with other casualties from the Saturday-night fire at the Pavilion. Cathy stopped the young woman doctor who had treated Paul.

"Excuse me," Cathy said. "I'm looking for Larry Hart."

"You're Cathy Malone," the doctor replied.

"Yes! Where's Larry?"

The doctor pointed toward a high white screen. "Over there. He's been asking for you."

"May I see him?" Cathy asked impatiently.

The doctor nodded. "Yes, but just for a moment. He's going to be all right, but I'll have to ask your friends to stay here."

Cathy glanced at Wendy, who smiled and told her to go on.

"Tell him we're pulling for him," Darren said.

Todd raised his fist in the air. "Steel forever."

Cathy turned away and hurried behind the screen. Larry was lying on a gurney with his eyes closed. Blisters dotted his face and hands. Most of his hair and both of his eyebrows had been singed off. He looked so horrible that Cathy was afraid to touch him.

She stood next to the gurney, gazing down at him. "Larry?"

His eyes flickered open. "Cat . . ."

"How do you feel?" Cathy asked.

"Hammered," Larry replied weakly.

"You're going to be all right. Everybody is pulling for you."

"Margo," Larry said in a raspy whisper.

Cathy nodded. "Yes, she set the fire. She killed Felicia and Paul."

Larry closed his eyes. He seemed so helpless. Cathy would have kissed him if he hadn't been covered with blisters.

"Cathy?"

She looked back to see the doctor. "Yes?"

"I think you'd better go. Larry's parents are on the way. He needs to rest now."

Cathy took one last look at Larry, then went to the waiting room to join the others.

"How is he?" Wendy asked.

"He's burned pretty bad, but he's going to make it," Cathy replied. "I wish I could stay with him."

Todd shivered. "We were lucky to get out of there alive."

Darren sighed. "The doctor says Larry is going to be here awhile. We can come back and visit him."

Wendy sighed deeply. "Well, at least Margo won't be here to push him off the roof."

Cathy began to cry. Wendy put her arms around her.

"You're coming home with me tonight," Wendy said. "You shouldn't be alone. We'll call your mother and tell her that you're okay, and then go to my place. Is that all right, Cathy?"

Cathy just nodded, sobbing softly on Wendy's shoulder.

Cathy sat on Wendy's bed, staring blankly at the television screen. The late news was reporting the Pavilion fire. Cathy grabbed the remote and turned off the television. She felt numb.

Wendy was in the bathroom next to the bedroom, washing her contacts. The door was open so she could talk to Cathy.

"How are you doing?" Wendy called over the sound of running water.

"Okay, I guess," Cathy replied. "My mom was glad to hear that I was all right. She had heard about the fire."

"I'm glad you're staying here tonight," Wendy said. "I feel creepy about the whole thing, even though my parents are here."

"Thanks, Wendy."

"You can stay in the guest room down the hall. Look in the third drawer of my dresser. There's a flannel nightgown in there."

Cathy thought Wendy had said the first drawer. Climbing off the bed, she went to the dresser and pulled open the top drawer. She began to look for the flannel gown in the neatly folded stacks of clothes.

"I don't see it," she called to Wendy.

"Look on the bottom."

Cathy dug into the drawer. Her fingers hit something cold and metallic. She pulled it out and stared at the two long, stainless-steel bolts in her hand. They were the bolts that had been removed from the drummer's platform at the junior-high gig.

Cathy's heart began to pound.

Cathy stared at the bolts in disbelief. Wendy was the one person she thought she knew, and now she realized that she hadn't known Wendy at all.

When Cathy heard Wendy coming back to the room, she shoved the bolts deep into her jeans pocket. Wendy came in, drying her hair.

"Wendy," Cathy began, "I've been thinking. Maybe I should just go home after all. Thanks for inviting me to stay, though." She grabbed her jacket and went quickly past Wendy.

"Wait a second, what are you doing? Don't you want a ride?" Wendy was looking at her in amazement.

"No, no," Cathy called, already down the stairs and at the front door. "I'll just walk." She was out the front door before Wendy could say another word.

Frigid November air rushed around her as she ran along the sidewalk. Even though she was wearing a jacket, Cathy immediately felt the effects of the cold on her chest and arms. She stopped for a moment, gasping in the night air.

Cathy turned, running through Rocky Bank Estates, heading for Pelham Four Corners. It was too late for the buses to be operating, so she would have to run the whole way to the Upper Basin. By the time she reached the Four Corners, her chest was on fire. Her body trembled and her legs were weak, but she had to keep going. All she wanted to do was get home.

Cathy sucked in cold air. Turning to the right, she staggered the few blocks to her house. The lights were off; her mother had gone to bed. Cathy paused in the driveway. She really had to think this through, figure out what to do.

Reaching for her back pocket, Cathy touched the key bolts. She had to hide them. She had to make sure the evidence was safe.

Moving past her house, she ran softly up the driveway to the garage. Her aching fingers worked the dial of the combination lock. It took her a minute to get the door open.

The garage was dark and cold inside. Cathy slid through the shadows, switching on the light over her sound board.

"I knew you'd come here!"

Cathy wheeled to see Wendy standing in the open doorway. "Get away from me, Wendy!"

"I took my father's car," Wendy said. "You didn't think I'd let you go, did you? Not after what you found out. Now, give me those bolts."

Looking across at her, she could see Wendy's eyes glittering unnaturally with suppressed excitement. Cathy slowly drew her breath in as she had a terrifying thought.

"You pushed Paul off the roof of the hospital." Cathy guessed quietly.

"You were going to let him back in the group," Wendy said coldly. "I didn't want that, Cathy. He was going to get in the way. We weren't going anywhere with Paul as our drummer."

"Felicia. Did you . . ." Cathy felt like she was going to faint with shock.

Wendy laughed. "Yes, I did Felicia. I set that cord. She was going after Todd. I couldn't have that. It would mess up the group."

Cathy stared into the black wells of Wendy's eyes. "You wanted Larry back in the group. You wanted us to stay together when we were all on the verge of quitting. How could you—"

"Larry was the best," Wendy replied. "We had a shot at the big time as long as Larry was on the drums. I realized that after I heard Paul. We needed Larry. We were so close to stardom, but then that idiot Margo had to pull her stupid stunt."

"You killed two people so the group would make it? That's sick, Wendy."

Wendy scowled at her. "You don't see, do you, Cathy? This group is my ticket out of Cresswell. I'm going to be a star. And we can still make it, Cathy. When Larry gets out of the hospital, we can put the group together again."

"No, Wendy, not like this."

"Yes! We'll be more popular than ever. People are fascinated by our bad-luck reputation. The news about Margo will be all over the papers and on television. I couldn't have planned it better myself. This is our ticket to the top."

Cathy stiffened, and shook her head. "No. I'm going to turn you in, Wendy."

Wendy smiled wickedly. "Who's going to believe you?"

Cathy held up the bolts. "The sheriff will, when I show him these."

Wendy reached for the stainless-steel ax that was hanging by the door. "I don't think so, Cathy."

Cathy's eyes grew wide. "All right, Wendy. You win. Here, take them." She threw the bolts at Wendy's feet.

A strange smile spread over Wendy's face. "No, that's not good enough anymore."

"What do you mean?"

"*I'm* going to tell the story," Wendy replied. "About how I found the bolts in your garage, about how you tried to kill me. They'll find you after I burn the place down. You'll be gone, and I'll be off the hook."

"You've lost it, Wendy. You have to turn yourself in. You'll be able to get some help."

"I don't need help," Wendy replied. "I just need you out of the way."

Cathy leaned back against the sound board. Her hand fumbled with the dials until she found the power switch. She turned on the board as Wendy came toward her.

"What if I don't tell, Wendy? What if I . . ."

"You know too much," Wendy replied. "It's all over now. Wouldn't that make a good song title? I can dedicate it to you."

Cathy's face tightened into a hateful sneer. "You won't dedicate anything to me, Wendy."

"What do you mean by that?"

"You're a coward," Cathy replied. "You sneak around, killing people. But I'm not afraid of you."

"You should be," Wendy said, frowning. "I have the ax."

"You can't kill me, Wendy."

Wendy nodded, her eyes glassy and distant. "Oh, I can kill you. Another death will be just what we need for Heart of Steel. We'll be the most famous band in the history of Cresswell. All thanks to you and Margo."

"Come on, then," Cathy said, waving her hand. "Come and kill me if you think you can do it, Wendy. You don't have the guts."

Wendy laughed maniacally. "I have the guts. Good-bye, Cathy. You were a real trouper. I'm going to miss you."

Cathy tensed as Wendy lifted the ax. When she brought the ax down, Cathy dove out of the way, hitting the floor. Wendy sunk the ax into the sound board, wedging it into the current of the electrical wires.

Wendy began to scream and then was choked into silence. The current flowed up the handle of the ax, biting her with two hundred and twenty volts. Her body twitched violently. The acrid smell of burning hair and flesh filled the garage.

Cathy watched in horror as Wendy's body shook. Finally, she tore her gaze away from the sight, rushed to the other side of the garage, and threw the main power switch. The current sparked and fizzled as it died.

Wendy slumped to the floor. Her eyes were still open and glassy. But when Cathy bent over the charred body, she knew that Wendy was dead.

Cathy sat across from Sheriff Hagen's desk, slumped on a ratty sofa. She had told him everything about Wendy. The sheriff was leaning back, staring out of the window.

She wasn't sure if Hagen believed her. She wondered if her mother would be disappointed in her. Cathy had never been in trouble, but now she seemed to be lost in a deep, dark pit.

The sheriff turned suddenly, looking at her. "Okay, Cathy, you can go."

"Just like that?"

He sighed. "I can't hold you. It's clear that the Coles girl was trying to kill you with that ax. How else could she have ended up like that?"

Cathy stood up. "Sheriff, before she died, she confessed that she had killed Felicia and Paul."

Hagen nodded. "I'll put that in my report. I may need you to testify in front of the grand jury, Cathy."

"Yes, sir. Thank you, Sheriff Hagen. Thank you for believing me."

"It's over now, Cathy. Isn't it?"

"Yes, sir. It's over."

When Cathy left the office, her mother was waiting for her outside. They embraced and started to cry. Cathy knew it was finished, but it wouldn't be over until the group gathered again in her garage.

Jack shook his head, frowning. "Man, Wendy really hacked that sound board to death."

Darren grimaced. "She hacked herself."

Cathy sighed, gazing toward the mess. "It doesn't matter now. I've just got to start over."

Jack shivered. "We all could've been charcoal if Wendy hadn't liked us. I can't believe it. I thought she was cool."

Someone knocked at the door of the garage. Todd Steele pushed through the doorway. They all looked at him. He looked down at his boots.

"Guess you guys don't want to see me," he said roughly.

"It's all right," Cathy said. "You didn't know about Wendy. Did you?"

Todd shook his head sadly. "She had me fooled, too." He looked tired and pale.

"We all came to help Cathy get it together," Jack replied. "How'd you know we'd be here?"

"I called him," Darren replied. "He's part of the group."

"I don't mind," Cathy said.

Todd gazed at the mangled sound board. "Wow. It's trashed."

Cathy shuddered at the memory of that night. It had taken her almost a month to find the courage to return to the garage. She could still see Wendy standing there, shaking with the current of death surging through her.

Jack smiled at her. "It's okay, Cathy. I'm here to help. We all are."

"Let's get it over with," Cathy said softly.

As they were moving toward the sound board, they heard a motorcycle pulling up outside. Jack turned to frown at the door. Larry was out of the hospital.

Cathy put her hand on Jack's shoulder. "I'm sorry, Jack, but Larry and I are going steady again."

Jack took a deep breath. "Aw, I—I'm okay, Cathy. Forget about it."

"Thanks, Jack."

Larry came in, shivering from the cold ride. His skin had healed for the most part, though there were still red splotches on his arms. He carried a brown grocery bag with him.

"It's cold out there," he said. "I thought I'd bring some coffee and—"

He stopped when he saw Jack.

Cathy moved next to Larry. "Jack came to help us."

Jack shook his head. "It's okay, Hart. I'm cool. Shake on it."

"Sure," Larry said. "No hard feelings."

When they had shaken hands, Larry turned toward the sound board, grimacing. "Wow, Wendy really did a number."

"I can rebuild it," Cathy replied.

"Let's get to work," Todd said. "I'd like this group to fly again."

Darren nodded. "Me, too. How about it, Cathy?"

Cathy shrugged. "Why not? We'll need a new singer."

"Let's do it," Jack said.

They started to work, clearing away the mangled mess. Even without the sound board, Cathy was able to get one of the amps working. She told Todd to plug in his guitar.

Todd held his breath and switched on the old Fender. "I don't even know if this will work."

"Give it a shot," Cathy said.

Todd struck a pose and hit the chord. The garage filled with a screeching riff of electric music. Everyone clapped.

"Rock and roll!" Todd cried.

Larry slipped his arm around Cathy's shoulder. "I love you, babe."

Cathy leaned against him. "I love you, too."

She looked at her sound board. It would take a while to get it back in shape, but she was ready to work again. She knew it was the only way to put all of the bad memories behind her.